FINANCIAL THRILLER

THE DEAD BANK DIARY

SERIES

I0537912

THE PRINTS ON THE SNOWS OF YESTERYEAR

By Anna Schlegel

BOOK THREE

Translation from Russian

Schlegel Press Association

The Prints On The Snows Of Yesteryear by Anna Schlegel
Book Three of The Dead Bank Diary Series

Published by Schlegel Press Association
Friedrichstr. 123
Berlin, Germany 10117

ISBN: 9780986174971

First Edition: November 2015

Translated by Alla Koshechkina
Cover photography Hemis /Alamy & Maxim Shirkov /Shutterstock

Also By Anna Schlegel

THE DEAD BANK DIARY SERIES

THE DEAD BANK DIARY

Book One of The Dead Bank Diary Series

FOR THOSE IN THE SHADE

Book Two of The Dead Bank Diary Series

SOME DAY I`LL HIT A BANK

Book Four of The Dead Bank Diary Series

THE FROZEN DEBT

Book Five of The Dead Bank Diary Series

MY GOD IS MONEY

Book Six of The Dead Bank Diary Series

Coming Soon

Also By Anna Schlegel
THE SLEEPER SERIES

MONEY CAN`T LIE

Book One of The Sleeper Series

ON MYSELF FOR LITTLE MONEY

Book Two of The Sleeper Series

Coming Soon

CONTENTS

AUTHOR'S NOTE

In these books there are no cops, no killings. There is much about the illegal takeover of banks, and a powerful lot of money. I know how to pump up a bank, and how to bankrupt a bank. I love beautiful gray schemes on the verge of crime. My stories are about fraud in the eyes of a swindler. There are no good guys.

I write about the golden-time bankers, from 1998, when neither the police nor the intelligence services, or any crimes haven't prevent the banks to make money.

These novels are not based on a true story, but you will face this reality in every word.

Anna Schlegel

The best to rob the bank is the banker himself

THE PRINTS ON THE SNOWS OF YESTERYEAR

The bank facing bankruptcy fell out of the hands like a snowball rolling downhill, flattening everything under its weight.

Behind every bankruptcy there are people who make it happen. But there are no influential people. Big figures are absent. It seems you stay face to face with the emptiness.

This happens when the Central Bank is playing against you.

ABOUT THE SERIES

These are stories about a man who is not alive anymore. He was a financier, a retired intelligence officer. I had the good luck to arrange a couple of financial frauds. We bumped into each other before the recession, in the flood of shit, together in the dust.

After his death I still had power of attorney.

Of course, Victor knew I wouldn't be able to work on his contacts. I had tried. Now it's funny to think of it. I am, and always have been, a go-between, a rat. Nobody needs middlemen. They get rid of them; they send them to Hell. But I had a white shirt with a necktie, and copies of million-strong contracts for oil, gas, diamonds, and rare-earth metals: light-as-air, rolled fax sheets with lots of zeroes. They made me giddy; they made me drunk. And I ran along with them, and easily foisted them for the middlemen: muddy, middle-aged misters.

When some of the first deals failed, I went into hysterics. I wanted to throw everything in.

Once I had a dream. In my dream, I heard a telephone call, – Miss Schlegel? We need your signature to extend a contract concluded by Mr. ...

I woke up scared; something turned over inside of me. I realized that I was spending my life waiting for such a call. It didn't matter where it caught me.

But there was no going back. Once you've taken a step forward, you realize you can't turn back anymore.

Why did he leave all this to me? I looked the papers over, recalling past years, deals, people, talks: everything from the first meeting to the last minute. And I couldn't find anything for me; because it wasn't for me, actually, for the old me. So I changed. I became a con.

My life was changed. Sometimes it was as convincing and disgusting as a life of a whore. It was as inaccessible as the man who despises you. It was like vomit or sweat from the body from heavy hangover shivers. You wish to run, and there's no place to run to. It's a cold stupor. So it's stupid to look at the smeared corpse on the road, and it's impossible to regain consciousness to look away. This passion nests in the heart, and you don't know what is it.

I have his photo, the last one, taken at Arkhangelskoe hospital. Summer. We're sitting on the edge of a dried-up fountain. He embraces me with one arm, and I'm lost next to him. He is gray-haired and corpulent. He has a mocking look. And behind us there are towering white marble angels.

CHAPTER ONE

THE BANKRUPT

Moscow, November 1999

Peter came back early. He came to the house and stayed on the doorstep. He smelled of snow, his sparse yellow teeth carried a smoldering cigarette. He did not take off his coat yet, the snow melting on his grey sprouted frizz, sticking to his wrinkled forehead. His soft and watery lose face seemed frozen.

"What happen, Peter?" I asked, shaking off the snow flakes from his coat collar, and taking the cigarette from his teeth for a pull.

"Ilya went bankrupt... By and by... rack and ruin..." he replied, looking away and picking out his cigarette from my suddenly stiffened fingers.

I had not expected this.

Ilya's bank was not making the top two hundred. It was what you call a pocket bank, formerly at the disposal of a major government company. Ilya became its chairman at first, in a nominal way. But over time the company left government custody, pulled its funds abroad, and the bank had eventually become Ilya's. He was running his business invisibly, for the most part, in Europe. He never intended to set it on any better path, and was keeping himself in shade.

However, this time Ilya had got it wrong. Peter and I, we had unwittingly stirred him to this.

It was a matter of a year and a half back, when Peter took the position of deputy chairman in Ilya's bank, and tried to take over the bank. I had slightly helped Peter. Ilya's bank was heavily in arrears and could hardly stay afloat; it appeared it hadn't been so difficult to get a hold of it. It seemed with just a bit more effort Ilya's bank would be in our hands. But Ilya managed to pledge Foreign Currency Bonds with some small European banks. Deutsche Bank issued him the bank guarantee against the bank securities of those hundred banks, so Ilya's bank received so much money it was impossible to approach.

But today those Foreign Currency Bonds had lost their value.

Our bank takeover had failed that time, but it had changed our lives. Peter's reputation was badly tarnished, and no bank would ever employ him. It was a shame since he actually was a born financier with a bulldog attitude. I had been jobless for a long time. Sometime in the past I used to be a trader in Securities, and resigned to run after multi-million-dollar business, until Peter picked me up like a stray cat, in my beaten up shoes with a hungry look.

Peter became just like me: a middleman in off-exchange trade. This kind of broker was considered the garbage of the market. We used to snatch at everything and anything without regard like two famished mongrels throwing themselves onto the bones left by the kitchen midden. They say buffalos would die of hunger and the hyenas would eat each other. No, this did not happen to us. Peter and I were hanging together like two bloaters, and the stronger the grip the less hope there was to get out of the shithouse, and we kept drowning there. Was it the misery holding us together? What could one earn in a dead market?

I had started looking at my reflection in the mirror more often lately, with attention and distance, examining my insipid and sharp face. Did it show I was moneyless? In the past, when I had an entire week of no transactions I was actually scared the sound of my voice would give me away, and it was clearly so. I actually used to notice it myself with the brokers I spoke with daily on the phone. I had a good antenna for money. The broker who can't make a deal makes people scatter as if he's a leper. And how much effort is required to hide the matter! So what will happen in a month time? I must have been wearing a – *No cash available, No cash...* – message across my forehead... I was looking at my reflection with the only thought, *Where can I hide that dead beat look?*

Peter and me, we were renting a two-room flat in the suburbs of Moscow, waiting for a chance to launch a raid on some other bank. This flat served us as a broker's office with a sole trader. There was nothing to hope for, however. Every morning, all week long except weekends, I was making porridge for Peter; we had breakfast together and parted to have our various appointments, and in the evening after dinner, we used to smoke thinking of what we could do the following day, and then each of us went to their bedroom.

On weekends I left for Ilya's house in the countryside. Sometimes Ilya sent a car for me midweek, and I joined him in his apartment. I had no business with Ilya. I just shared a bed with him.

Ilya was seventy, but neither he nor I, nor anyone else who used to know him would ever sense his age. In the market they used to say, Ilya had buried four of his deputies, and just caught a cold himself.

I could not refuse my meetups with Ilya and did not want to get any closer to him either. There were too many reasons. Ilya had been by himself all along. I did not want to be a burden for him. For a long time I had a feeling of Ilya's being tired, and too tired to kick me aside. But then I realized he found me easy to be with. Me and Peter, we used to get into all kind of crap, and I wouldn't wish Ilya to get into the same. I equally did not want Ilya to think of what I had stepped into. He had an entire shithouse to himself, actually. So he did not worry about me, as if he wanted me to have that crap to my heart's content. In the post-crisis stock-market there was enough of that crap to go around.

Initially it seemed to me that Ilya and me, we were far too different people. But nope, we were similar, as if as they say, we used to piss in the same pot as kids. I must have inherited my father's old-fashioned manners. Ilya used to tell me he could not shake the feeling he was speaking to me like to my father.

My father once told me, wincing as if he had a sore mouth, that he would be happy to talk to Ilya late in life, sitting in the diapers on a bench...

In a prison-yard, I used to joke.

In fact it was too late to change things. Ilya said, *We are late, baby.*

I was leading my own way, and Ilya was going his.

Who would have known the Foreign Currency Bonds would lose their value?

There was a collapse.

No one expected it to happen. The major Russian banks used to take out loans secured by government stocks, Foreign Currency Bonds, Eurobonds and obligations to the London Club. All of these had depreciated in a blink, to a mere ten percent of their face value. Our banks were, in a minute, losing hundreds of million dollars with this collapse. And the European banks concurrently called for additional payment of these stock values that were marked to the market and depreciating.

Eventually, Ilya lost over two hundred million dollars.

So he just did not have any funds. And he could not have any. His bank had no working capital at all.

Deutsche Bank, having realized it, with no chance of winning a lawsuit, took a decision to assign the right to recover Ilya's debt to another Russian bank, namely F-Group, and proposed Ilya take a merger with that bank.

Ilya did his best playing for time with his bank failure. His salvage for a while was in the moratorium on payments to non-resident banks. Still he had no chance to escape bankruptcy.

In the sober light of day, none of Ilya's key creditors, who were five small-scale defense industry enterprises, had no intention to drive him to bankruptcy. Ilya gathered his creditors and they took a decision to discard the bankruptcy, and signed for an amicable settlement with the bank. But this solution could satisfy neither Deutsche Bank nor the Central Bank.

Ilya himself had never enjoyed good relationship with the Central Bank. But F-Group bank, to whom Deutsche Bank was ready to assign the right to recover the debt, actually had rather good relationship with the Central Bank.

Basically, Ilya had to accept a merger with F-Group, who had already started making the paperwork ready.

"Have you seen Ilya?" I asked Peter, looking into his troubled face, where a flurry of thoughts seemed over-run by a ripple of wrinkles.

"Yeah. Ilya has appointed me vice-chairman in one of the banks. Not a bank actually, but a shithouse incidentally still holding its license."

"Why does Ilya need that bank then?"

"No idea. One of its shareholders has transferred the management of his parcel of shares to Ilya.

The rest Ilya has taken as lien, real cheap. Who would refuse?"

"So what did Ilya say?"

"He told me to knock the bank into shape, told me to boost the charter capital. No problem. But I find it a shame to be even asking for money for such a bank. One is ashamed to ask people in, actually. It's a dog-hole office. I'm a horse's ass with my teeth missing. Who would be talking to me? I told Ilya, *Give me some cash to place a golden ashtray in the meeting room, at least.* And he wouldn't. He's got no cash!"

"Why this ashtray?" I did not get him.

"It's simple. A wealthy client comes to see a gilded ashtray. Then I take him to my friend's bank, there is a similar gilded ashtray. The client gets to think I have opened a branch office, and plunks down his money."

"Can you ever meet such dummies really?" I smiled.

"It's not hard work to place an ashtray... "

"What's this F-Group?" I snapped at Peter.

"I don't know. Why this particular F-Group? The Central Bank wanted it this way," Peter stretched out for a cigarette.

Having a smoke after Peter, I was thinking for the whole of my relationship with Ilya to be over. There was nothing out of the ordinary; I had been meeting Ilya at the porch of his country house. I could no longer do without these dates. And from now on, there seemed be no more of these. The bankruptcy would kill the little we had together. Everything around me appeared to be as fragile as glasswork. As if a glass incidentally flew out of my hands with all of its contents spilling, and smashed into smithereens.

A wave of hunger came to my throat, as it usually was when Ilya left.

"So how is Ilya himself?" I asked catching myself asking about Ilya as if I had not seen him a while, and had little chance of seeing again.

"Ilya is sinking, and dragging everyone with him. He's doing real bad. Everyone is scattering from him as if he were plague-stricken," Peter said in a softer tone, smoothing out his wrinkled forehead like ceasing crease marks on the water. "He

21

wants to go Switzerland to speak to each of his creditors privately... And who would let him go to Switzerland with that much debt? His feet-first only."

CHAPTER TWO

THE BERLIN BANK

Where to get funds from in the graveyard market?

Every day of mine started the same,

"Anna. How do you do. What's the update on your bank bills today?"

I used to ask this question over fifty times a day, ringing round the banks and companies that were in the Securities market. I used to buy and sell bank bills and debts from various companies. And then there were only debts available in the market. And I was dead tired of empty pocket and all this running around for nothing. And with all my effort I could make would just slip through my fingers anyway.

I'd intended to sit down at my telephone as usual, and could not, killing the clock and fooling around, flitting through my notes with debt quotations. I crossed out a dozen of offers and marked in red the urgent ones, and then put them all aside. For another ten minutes I kept staring blankly at an order application for a hundred thousand tons of oil. This one was nice. It was so nice. It was half past ten. I had been losing time already; one should not be looking at the same paper for such a long time. It was high time to palm it off on someone.

And then suddenly I thought, *Where the hell did this one come from?* And then I realized the market had changed. This kind of request used to run in the market three years back.

I made another couple of calls. Everything seemed to be just the same as usual. The market was no market, a crashing bore. It was bargains out of courtesy, never conceding half a percentage point, at fixed prices. No pleasure at playing fast and loose. The voices were dull and words were hollow. But then I suddenly scented something familiar, something of the times prior to default. Or had I mistaken it for something? What was it? Where did it come from so clear and sweet, just like of oven-fresh bread from the bakery on a frosty day, from a few quarters away?

I did not pick up my phone anymore. It was clear I would not call a single bank anymore and wouldn't speak to any more brokers. I still could not trust myself, sitting at the table facing my fax, looking vacantly at my own notes. And then I swept them up into a waste-basket.

The telephone kept silent, as if it were dead. The market had died.

Half-vacant buses were running along the empty highway. The city looked somber and shabby in those deserted lonely streets. And faces of the people passing by were somewhat stiff, tired, and hateful. One could immediately notice the aged faces. The daily accumulated impotent rage was pouring into crime news, platitudes, impudent lies, criminal argot and hardcore porn. And everything rotten through the Soviet times had come to stick out all round the place with its ugly misery, just like totally decomposed human remains coming out of the melting snow in springtime. The little acquitted over ten years of freedom has suddenly shelled off.

Moscow was paralyzed. The money ran dry; there was no more. The banks went bankrupt one after another, and the investment companies closed down, and those remaining were busy with encashment. All days long thousands of cash counting machines kept rustling in the tiny cubicles rented by minor banks and companies in the large hall of the exchange house. How funny and antediluvian it was! Formerly when making calls to Irkutsk to sell something, I could hear through the conversation this continuous chirrup of a dozen machines counting banknotes. And it was the only place they used to operate large volumes of cash. And now the same chirrup and rustle of notes filled the city of Moscow.

My telephone kept silent for days. My fax machine didn't squeak for more paper. For quite a long time I found it hard to get used to my phone being silent. One could go deaf with its muteness. This deafening silence initially seemed annoyingly persistent, dull and pointless, and then I turned indifferent to it.

There was deep frost outdoors, exceeding twenty below zero. The air seemed clear, transparent, still and bitterly cold, like a glass of pure alcohol. Peter and I drove to the bank office, the one that for no apparent reason had fallen into his hands.

In the boulevard there were bare trees, with gravel paths shining through, dirty pink just like the color of skin. Further on there was a muddy pond in ripples, full-brimmed with the reflection of the grey houses on the other side. Shredding them to pieces, came floating a white and shivery ice. At the footbridge there wheeled a flock of grey ducks, totally grey just like everything around, the buildings and the waterside concrete.

On the dirty façade above the closed doors there was blinking in dirty blue neon light the signage 'The Berlin Bank'.

"The Berlin Bank? The bank name is Berliner?" I asked in surprise. "Why not Barclays right away?"

"Oh, don't you tell me of Barclays bank. It has shown a profit of four million. With all the credit lines from the Arabs. So pulling down all those credit lines of forty to sixty billion and getting four million end of the year?! Too funny. To project the year-end profit of four million! To zero out the balance, that is..." Peter could keep on grumbling for ages. "And, talking of the Arabs. I do need a gilded ashtray," he smiled his toothless grin, looking at the bank signage. "This bank was once registered in a town of Berlin in Siberia. Its owner opened a branch in Moscow and went broke. That's the only thing remaining of the bank: a mere name."

The bank was actually finished off. It was no different from a cheap café in Chinatown, where I used to sit all day with a cup of coffee with the same kind brokers just like me. Neither me, nor any of them had any office.

It was dark in the anteroom.

At the door Peter was greeted by a plumpish gentleman of about forty with a satiated white face. He started talking right away, in a pushy and relaxed manner. He was well dressed, somewhat stylish. His suit was a thousand dollars. He was wearing Gucci shoes. The most expensive kind worm by Moscow gangsters engaged in business. His black hair was slicked back on one side, with a white parting line unwittingly drawing the eye. He could pass for a car spare parts dealer. His manners were quite pleasant, broad and smooth.

"Serge," he presented himself.

I scanned his face once again and my glance froze at his shoes. He was a middleman, just like Peter and me.

When Peter entered, his bookkeeper took him aside.

"You may start without me. You don't mind?" Peter said and nodded to the conference room in the depths of the long and narrow corridor.

The doors of the open offices made it look like a compartment car.

"So what do you come with?" I asked dully, inviting Serge to take a seat, and looking over the conference room I thought a gilded ashtray would actually come in handy.

"An asset," he uttered with a sweet crackle in his voice. "An illiquid one. And it is controlled by five, -six companies. Not for sale. But in case one needs to make his money work, anything may serve a turn. It can be taken in hand, taken and laid on the table. So that, there is a task to ensure a flow of funds. And a possibility to set up an asset. I'll name it. The asset is up-market. And potentially long-playing... "

He was speaking at length and quite thoroughly. His pleasant voice was nice to hear.

"So how much have you got?" I finally asked.

"250 grams."

I should have asked right away. Stupid me. I was trading in the same back in 1996.

Had the market put the clock back five years back? Or further back? Where do these brokers get that bad seller crap? I would not be surprised to see the gem-stones come. Someone would open up his safe deposit box, wipe the dust off his two-kilo ruby, and restart the running on the market therewith.

"Selenium?"

There used to be a lot of selenium on the market at that time. Its world consumption was apparently 7 kilograms, I think. As for us... Now and then some troubled brokers used to bring us ink-stamped documents, in a humble way, for 100 or 200 grams each. And there appeared to be no buyer. While of course it could still work as a financial instrument.

"Yes," he felt bad about these talks getting finished so fast.

"No, thank you. I don't find it acceptable for us; I guess Peter Petrovich thinks the same."

I saw him at the door, come back and double up exhausted on the sofa, crying quietly with dry eyes.

Peter used to tell me to stay away from any idiots who would draw us into their troubles and feed on. Idiot-immunity goes down in particular when you are not feeling well, they seem to have an antenna for this and crawl out of the woodwork, hooking onto you as if getting rescued from the underworld. No wonder! Anyone else in my place would have sent this Serge to Hell from the start. And I could not. And he knew it.

"Peter, what do you think, who is this Serge?" I asked Peter when he looked in the doorway. "A quarterdecker? Have you seen that suit of his! And his shoes? Gucci."

"Yeah, too much of a smart-ass," Peter agreed. "He'll get himself shot, dressed in a Hugo Boss and buried..."

"Where are they coming from now?" I wondered under my breath.

"By the way, got to find out on that F-Group from Victor. Let's call him. There is only one major account with Ilya's bank: Union-Reserve company. The company's money lies idle in the bank correspondent accounts in Switzerland. Ilya won't ever touch it and will manage to withdraw it in case of default. I think that F-Group intends to dive their hand into these accounts, and get hold of that client. And they've got an arrangement with the Central Bank already. We got to know who stands up for F-Group," Peter snorted and went into his pocket for the cell. "Hello Victor. Have you heard something of the F-Group?"

Victor's voice was remote and indifferent,

"Argh... F-Group? That's Anton... Erm...Anton has got a wife, Natalia, a blonde... locks and looks, holy boobs, stunning. He was on a visit to South Korea; imagine the reception with Natalia standing in the doorway. And the Koreans, all of them so small and skinny. In a word, a waiter bringing in aperitif drinks stares at her and can't take his eyes off her, and she's turning to him with her full-fledged boobs. His tray went flying. And one of the glasses stuck in her breast, in décolletage... There is always something like that happening to Natalia."

"So how could Anton stay up?" Peter inquired in perplexedly.

"He was working under diplomatic cover. And the embassy people knew it. You could say it! It was all clear. The car and gifts…"

"So how did he take hold of that bank?"

"Natalia has been sleeping with someone in the President's administration," simply said Victor.

"And Anton is making business with that?"

"You could lay a platoon on her boobs," and we heard his distant laughter. "Who's got to know about Anton? Is Ann there?"

"Yes."

"Pass her the phone," Victor asked. "Are you still with Ilya, honey bunny?"

"Yes."

"Why have you taken to Ilya? Has he finally remembered the Communist Party account numbers?"

"Nope."

"So what are you doing with the old man? Giving him a clyster?"

"No."

"Come to me, I'll fuck you," he told me ritually, as if asking, how are things?

"Hope you are doing well, too. And no, thanks. Victor, I've got to know who is the true owner of F-Group, that's all."

"I can't promise, Bunny," Victor dropped, saying goodbye.

"You know what, go see your father, he might know Anton," Peter said after some thinking.

CHAPTER THREE

ARCADY

My father lived nearby Barrikadnaya metro station. I entered the precinct. A spotted dog at the gateway sprinkled with snow was getting warm on the heated cast-iron manhole cover.

Arcady used to have visitors all the time, sometimes in crowds throbbing in the smoke from one room to another. Some of them smoked on the stair landing. Arcady knew all of Moscow's *beau-monde*, and now from time to time was trading with his contacts, putting down a telephone number on a piece of paper and giving it away sometimes for a thousand dollars, sometimes for a better sum. If someone had ever told him that his former position of vice-director in one of Yeltsin's corporations could make him a financial match-maker trading in telephone numbers of his former acquaintances to earn his living, he would have never believed it. Most of the time he was getting just pocket money. Friendship has stopped being the driving force for decision-making in business. It was now all about money.

It was all downtrodden in the corridor, and the wet footprints were stretching into the depths of the corridor, a row of empty vodka bottles was lining against the wall. Well, at this time Arcady did not have too many guests.

In the doorway there was Igor, his face red and sodden with booze taking up the entire doorway. Taking a cigarette each, we stood together in the door landing. His eyes, red as ever, *burnt with napalm,* as Arcady used to joke about him, narrowed straining to see me through the blurry film. He had his neck wrapped in a thin scarf and his grey topcoat collar up, his beefy stout body getting lost there. He was an ex-intelligence officer, an old friend of mine.

"Look, Anna," blooming his stinky booze-breath over me, he took me under the elbow to face him. "The Kazakhs came to me; they've got a gold mine valued at two million dollars. So, they want as security... "

"The subsoil is no storage depot, one can't really pledge it," I laughed mildly, thinking that Igor must have lost himself into drinking.

"They issued promissory notes for that sum;" he lost my laughter on the wind. "They require a Safekeeping Receipt from any bank, be that on the verge of license revocation. And my foreign partners offer for that matter a letter from UBS."

"Really? Are you serious?"

"Why, don't you trust me?" turning red in the face and neck, he tore at me out of a clear sky.

I just shrugged, and had a puff, hiding my eyes behind the smoke, avoiding eye contact. I had no wish to touch him over trifles. But I had no wish to listen to him speaking either. There was too much idle talk here. But then, bending over so that I felt hot and drunk with his face, and looking straight into my eyes, he hissed spitefully through his teeth:

"I've got a timber-toe, wanna me to unstrap it?"

"Oh, skip it. So what's there exactly?"

"Well," his face backed away, pressing me no more. "What we need is a letter of intent from any bank, even with its license to be revoked in a month's time. What we make is a reconfirmation for that Safekeeping Receipt. That's all. You got it? We need a bank that agrees. The bankers fail to understand what we want. They say, *Eh... What about money? We will credit you there!* Hell no. We need no money. And the talks come to deadlock."

"Yep, with a bubble taking shape the bankers get to run away pretty fast," I burst out laughing again.

"Oh yeah, and I've got to run now. By the way, my interest in that deal is actually good. And meanwhile, could you lend me a hundred rubles?" he asked ritually as if among other things.

"No."

Fedor Andreevich promptly came up to us, small and fat as a feeder pig, with a bristle of rare white hair on his sleek pink bare patch, that from afar seemed to be sprinkled with ashes:

"Those promissory notes are useless papers," he dropped on his way, holding out his plump hand to Igor who shook it blindly, "until they are confirmed by a normal bank for a ruble worth. And then, what are you talking about? Gold mines? Good gracious, what have we come to! What have we come to!" Fedor Andreevich said at the exit, and the grumbling echo brought his words under the ceiling of the stair landing.

"Fedor Andreevich," I caught him by his sleeve. "Do you happen to know something about Anton from F-Group?"

"Sure. He's got a wife... Natalia, plump and white... a sex bomb in a word. I was on my business trip to South Korea, came to a banquet reception, the Koreans could not take their eyes off her. There was fish getting served, a huge fish cut into pieces just per the number of guests. So each of the guests was served a portion. There remained a head and a tail on the dish. And Natalia wanted some more. She leaned across the table and reached out her breast for the fish with a fork and knife, all of the Koreans looking up and down, and one of them cried out pitifully, Madam that's a moulage!"

"A moulage?"

"Yes, and a nice one, you wouldn't tell. That is to show what kind of dish was there, to fill the empty platter on the table... Well, see you."

And Fedor Andreevich groaned making his way down the stairs. The guests smoking on the landing wistfully followed with their eyes his bald head descending into the bottom of the somber flight as a plunker in the cigarette smoke hanging in the air behind that darkness like a fog over the lake. What were they thinking of? Oh, that thing, *What have we come to!*

Indeed, we have come to the gold mines there. Trading in that crap actually was actually losing self-respect. Today self-respecting businessmen would not moon over millions, but rather count up one hundred banknotes. Everyone used to account in millions up to the crisis of 1998, millions and billions, thousands of oil tons, gold and diamonds, federal programs... Who would trade in these days?

I remembered the years prior to the crisis, and suddenly felt pain and sorrow, for no particular reason. And found myself incidentally thinking,

The winter will be long.

I entered the apartment and called for Arcady; my voice appeared to be lost in the depths of the corridor.

Arcady was just like a father to me. He has been with me since my childhood years, always there, after my father's descent. I was a copy of Arcady's and never tried to be anything else.

Arcady turned out right in front of me, quiet and silent.

"Hi," looking at me, Arcady somewhat relaxed.

Only here time would stop for me. As if all those crazy years had never happened. And everything here remained the same as in my early years.

"So what are you doing, Dad?"

"You remember Alexander Vassiliev? He came to me a week ago, said he needed the money badly. I felt a pity for the old man," Arcady started telling me. "We dropped in several banks with him in vain. Some pocket change was given out of respect for him only. And he spent it on something the same day, and the next day called me in the morning and said he was in his full dress uniform with his car ready at the porch, intending to go to any bank where he could get some more cash. Just like a baby, by god!"

We laughed.

"So this is what I came to, I realized the name of Vassiliev is still worth something, and decided to sell the man himself; I thought why not to sell that name of his."

"His name?" I wondered. "But how can you sell a name, Arcady?"

Good gracious! What only we have not sold out there. But selling a name... That was just like trading in the prints on the snows of yesteryear. What was that octogenarian worth? Who would buy the old man? Who would need him?

"Today they are talking a lot of conciliation with the Germans. So I decided to arrange for the old man Vassiliev a proper Veterans' Movement," Arcady said. "By the way, there came a letter for him from Germany. There is a charity foundation ready to raise the matter. Thus, we firstly register this Veterans Movement and then celebrate the Victory day, invite some old folks, make a concert, serve vodkas...a hundred grams each. So, let's get started?"

CHAPTER FOUR

THE OLDEN NAME

I thought I'd better not tell Arcady about Ilya's bank pending bankruptcy. Arcady did not want to hear of Ilya.

"Ilya needs money," I whispered, awaiting his reproach.

"We are speaking of money, actually," responded Arcady, turning sulky.

The old man Vassiliev, Lieutenant General of the Air Force, treated Arcady in a featherlike manner, and Arcady also got to like him in his own way. Vassiliev kept doing his best to raise money for his Military electronics research institute. What to do? The research institutions were left decapitated, abandoned and void, with those empty corridors filled with nimble ambiguous people bustling in and out in pursuit of something else to sell.

Vassiliev has had all of it: the prosecution, search and seizure, investigations and courts. He would not stop for a minute. He had been at war, been to prison together with Korolev, has known Gagarin in person. At some time in the past he had been Head of Combat Aviation Department.

"That time, the deputy assistant secretary of Tupolev was invited for airborne radar system research two line-crossers from the USA... " Arcady told me.

"Line-crossers?" I asked again in surprise. "Spies, that is?"

"Yes, they became the forbearers of the microelectronics industry. And the first radar-controlled air defense weapons."

Joseph Berg and Philip Staros, the spies, used to be once upon a time Joel Barr and Alfred Sarant. This was one of those rare occasions of committed espionage, one in a thousand. Berg and Staros were offered money which they refused. What did they want then? They wanted to balance the powers? God only knows. Anyway, that time they were far from understanding how complicated was the espionage mechanism. And it actually was the way that getting incidentally a foothold into a gear would totally draw you in the flywheel, and if not grind you down, would sweat you up down to the ground, and if ever let you go, would be your feet-first or into prison, through the corridors of humiliation if not torment. And people used to get out broken-down and disemboweled, and in either event disillusioned. And once there came an ideological dreamer... Joel Barr and Alfred Sarant were no spies in its true meaning, as is normally the case, so the mechanism of professional espionage remained shielded for them; this is why they must have survived for such a long time.

In 1950 they were incidentally found, once a cryptogram of their intercepted correspondence was unclassified. The Lubyanka resolved to take them to Moscow. Joel Barr initially went to France and then to the Czechoslovakia, where he lived undercover as an engineer from South Africa. There he fell in love with a Czech woman named Vera, married her and then moved to Moscow. The Bergs had four children, but then he and Vera divorced after twenty years of married life together. Another two children were born to Berg by another woman at the time when everybody else turned back on him.

Alfred Sarant at the time a father to two children, suddenly fell in love, and left with his beloved Carol Dayton, also a mother to two children, following through Mexico, Morocco, Spain, and Poland. After some time Carol wanted to come back, but being accused of espionage by American government she had no way back. The fate of spies has permanently tied them together. The hundred per-center American Carol became Anna Petrovna, a humble wife of a Greek communist Philip Staros.

They both started to work with Tupolev.

Tupolev looked at the sample they brought and asked what they wanted to launch the project. Staros said they required qualified professionals, a hundred and fifty staff, and a production facility of six hundred square meters. Tupolev picked up his phone and dialed Khrushchev via direct line, telling they found professionals capable of engineering a compact airborne computer.

Khrushchev asked what they wanted. Tupolev turned to Staros and asked him once again,

"How much staff do you need?"

"One hundred and fifty people," reconfirmed Staros.

"A thousand and a half pax," reported Tupolev to Khrushchev, and turned to Staros again, "And how much floor?"

"Six hundred square meters."

"Six thousand square meters," reported Tupolev to Khrushchev.

"Well," responded Khrushchev, "make ready a draft decree of the Central Committee and Council of Ministers."

So firstly there was created a design engineering bureau near Leningrad, and then in Zelenograd province of Moscow there was launched an electronics research center.

Joel Barr went back to America in the 1990-s, stayed there for a while, but then left. He came back and died in Moscow at the age of eighty-one in 1998.

Arcady rented an office in an old building in the downtown, with windows looking to a booming yard tightly walled with the dirty behind of a few other houses.

We climbed the narrow staircase with steep stairs between humid chilly walls to the beaten door. Arcady opened the door into the blinding whiteness of a modest office. The walls painted in white and the bright daylight lamps dazzled the eyes. Except for the relative absence of furniture there was a table, a computer, a coffee-maker and some chairs.

"So who else is working on this with you?" I asked, staring at a pair of chairs by the table.

"Nobody else."

"Excellent! So no one to share the profit with!"

CHAPTER FIVE

THE SHUTTLE

We managed to achieve not so much that day. Arcady was taking his coffee thinking what to start with, and seemed to spend the whole day over a blank sheet of paper, where he wanted to draft a list of the future board for his Veterans' Movement.

The founders' list had to be headed by the Presidential Administration, several monopolists, major banks and reputable foundations. All of them were to get enrolled at once upon official request from the Presidential Administration.

I was calling round my contacts, those who could be of any assistance in that matter, and then ran out to the metro station to meet with Maxim. We took a bottle of beer each and started wading through the melting snow along the boulevard.

"Max, I wrote to the Ministry of Justice to get the Veterans' Movement registered."

"Who are the members?" Max inquired at once.

"Firstly, we'll just list them all on paper. Then we could call some of them to tell they are leaders of the Veterans Movement. Well, better never call, why? We'll add to the Founders list only those who appear in the news quite often, you got me?"

"No," Maxim cut me short unexpectedly.

"Which part don't you understand?"

"You never tell anyone they are leaders of the Veterans' Movement. What if they ever get to know that? Bring an action?"

"When they get to know, that'll be pretty late. And then we will be having a full-fledged Movement, and being its founder won't be a shame. Name-dropping may bring us business people with cash and the banks. In the case someone takes offence we will duly apologize. Some veteran would go to him, and say sorry he'd got things mixed up due to sclerosis, you got it?"

"No, I am not getting it," Maxim was getting obstinate, and started to scratch the back of his head and pulling his hair that tumbled out in plumes from under his fingers.

"Oh my god, Max!" I hissed angrily, "Which part don't you understand?"

"Which legal persons have you made terms with?"

Facing his glare for a moment I felt the pinprick of his tiny pupils on my skin.

"None at all, Max," deadly weariness came on me from Max's stupidity. "I'm here trying to come to terms with *you*, and you're being obstinate. That's a beginning. From zero."

"That smacks of delusion," Max clucked his tongue. "We need real members. They might require you to produce the minutes of the foundation meeting and the members' presence."

"They'd be all abroad... " I shrugged with a chilly cold feeling, either due to the cold beer, or due to the cold-blooded and precise description of the matter given by Max.

"Then you might fail to obtain the registration. Will your founders provide money?"

"Sure they won't! They are quite wealthy people! The money will be given by those who wish to stand by their side in this list. Why should we show bare ass out there?!"

"Ann, but that's a fraud... "

My boots were soaking. The cold water leaked to the tip of the toes and they were frozen up. The chilly crap of a beer stuck in my stomach. The conversation was turning out annoying.

"So why are you being obstinate, Max? Sure that's a fraud. No one but you and I could make it... "

"Me and you? Are you standing alone out there?" asked Maxim finally making something clear for himself.

I shifted my glance to Maxim's shoes and saw them thoroughly soaked. Maxim was standing as good as barefoot in the chilly water. No wonder this conversation could nothing but displease him, he just wanted to end these talks, to get into the warm insides of the Tube, that's it. I actually saw his soaking shoes leave the trace on the Tube's tiled floor, getting mixed with the traces of other people's.

He might have expected me to name the dignitary executives of the Presidential administration. But my toes were totally frozen up in my soaking boots. I could not divest myself of the idea of getting to the office, taking of those boots, placing my feet onto the hot radiator and taking a hot cup of coffee.

"No, there is Arcady."

"My god! There is Arcady! You should have told me earlier! Bye-bye, my dear."

Maxim wrapped up his coat and stepped out for the Tube. A melted medley sprayed out from under his shoes.

I came back to my office, took my boots off, placed them on the radiator, where I also put my feet, and bogged in hot coffee made by Arcady.

An hour passed, then another hour. We almost did not talk. The daylight lamps were buzzing obtrusively giving no chance to concentrate, and blinding me with their flecks. When looking up, I was facing the unbearable white of Arcady's shirt and his dry hands going through the white paperwork.

"You might ditch it all, you know that?" said Arcady putting aside some paper with tired gesture.

He dumped his cigarette butt into the heap of butts, and took another cigarette.

"Yeah, that may slip out," I agreed, also taking a smoke. "Have you got any other options?"

"No."

Arcady jumped to his feet, and started pacing up and down, measuring his office with his long legs.

"Then, could you do it yourself, Arcady?"

"No way, my dear."

I shrugged him off, tired of looking at his blinding white shirt beating up and down the wall and flashing in white patches, reflected in the dull polished surface of the table like lumps of melting ice in the muddy water.

"Here's the deal, I firstly call to Gafin, Alfa-Bank and tell him Pavlovsky wants to see him to talk over the Veterans' movement. Then I call Pavlovsky and tell him, there is Gafin who wants to see him. That's it. They would not meet either of us, but they would wish to see each other. We won't see money from them, but their support will get covered by other banks. That's a shuttle trade," I picked up the phone and hardened with the receiver in my hand for a minute, fumbling for words, my fingers running with sweat.

"You're an idiot," Ilya was standing on the threshold, and it seemed he had understood what the matter in question was. "You are idiots, both of you."

Ilya had a rigid face that appeared even whiter and more transparent under the lamplight. His grey eyes burned as cigarette ashes seemed unnaturally pale, his gaze being stony and vacant. His lips, slightly smiling, were firmly set as if frozen with the cold. Every line on his face was cut into this stiffened face like a crack on the ice.

"How do you do, Ilya," Arcady offered his hand in reluctance.

Ilya put a bottle of cognac on the table, took off his coat and jacket, adding the white of his shirt on the bowed stony shoulders.

"Give me your list, Arcady; I'll see what can be done."

He took the papers Arcady swept from the table, and leaning over them, he said,

"Put it down, Arcady," and Ilya gave five surnames.

Arcady put them down. The list contained all the right people, one from each group. One member from the Presidential administration, another from the Security Council, one from the City Hall, a Deputy Minister and an official from the federal financial industrial group.

"It's a close circle of good friends, of high profile. You won't need anyone else. And all of them old men," remarked Ilya.

"I got you," Arcady nodded taking the list.

We spent another couple of hours together. I was smoking, making coffee without taking a seat as I liked to lean into Ilya's face. But now I was not looking at him, scared to see his alien, cold stare. I had the impression he could be looking at me as if saying good bye.

Ilya looked through the draft letters made by Arcady for the governors and heads of administration in different regions and municipalities, the letters to the Presidential administration, different ministries, departments, foundations abroad, representative offices and embassies. Following Ilya, Arcady also made up a list of banks from which sponsorship could be requested.

"And what is there from the German side?" Ilya asked.

"The Veterans Charity Foundation, all of them old people," Arcady laid out the letters in front of him.

"We'll get the money to go through them," Ilya looked at Arcady questioningly, and the latter nodded.

Ilya stopped speaking. I felt uncomfortable. I was suddenly thinking that Ilya would not come like that in the middle of a business day, for nothing. He had never paid me and Peter a visit, and actually called us rarely. I looked at Arcady, and he had the same look.

"Ilya, why hell have you come?" Arcady asked.

"You must have heard I'm bankrupt?" Ilya responded unwillingly, and stood up putting on his jacket. "I've got to go to Switzerland."

"But how? You won't be released with so much debt."

"I know. So I need a guarantor and the security."

The silence appeared permanent. Ilya was looking into Arcady's eyes.

"And so why are you looking at me that way?"

Arcady's voice shivered, suspecting no good.

"You are the guarantor, and Ann – the security."

CHAPTER SIX

THE SECURITY

"Ilya, have you gone mad there?" Arcady cried out, his face momentarily convulsed like a stone thrown into still water.

Behind the windows there was a black early evening, due to those lights all around. The darkness seemed blinding against the lamplight and those white walls. The city behind the windows was quiet as it may only be on a winter's night after heavy snowfall. The snow was falling in rare, bulgingly big snow-flakes, flashing under the street light like golden coins, plenty of golden coins, and slipping by the window it dissolved into the darkness.

"I can't go just like that. That would look like a getaway. I want all of my creditors know that I have Anna, and that I'm coming back. Just in case, I will sign my apartment and my country house over to her; that is worth about twenty million dollars, so that she might sell and distribute the same among the creditors in case I don't come back," Ilya said simply.

"And what happens to her in case you are not back?" Arcady was still screaming.

"Nothing happens. All of my creditors are directors of major defense enterprises and friends of mine. Nobody kills her. The maximum in store for her is becoming someone's mistress. But I won't know about it, if it happens: that would mean I'am already dead. Arcady, have I told you, you are coming with me to Switzerland?" asked Ilya.

They both kept silent. That was a strange conversation. I felt bad with Ilya's talking like that.

"Ilya, so you don't know what happens to me in case you are not there anymore? Or you know that? Or you don't want to know? Shall I tell you?" I asked.

"Please don't, baby," Ilya screwed up his face.

"I'll tell you. Nothing will change. I'll continue living as I do, together with Peter. You are never around. I am getting into all kind of shithouses, straining on my phone to ask you, *How shall I get on?* And then I realize you've got far more important things to consider. Peter always got the time for me. It would be silly to think I'm there looking forward to your offer to live together. You don't really think I'm waiting for you out there, do you?"

"No, I don't," Ilya nodded.

"You once said we are actually too late to be together. And I was still waiting for something, waiting for you to change your mind. And then I stopped waiting. I understood, everything will remain as it is, limited to some weekends with you, that's it. You have never even asked if I wanted to be with you all the time. And, God kill me, I don't know what to do with you all week long. You wouldn't wish me to use the landline to sell rare metals or diamonds in the market. I am not waiting for you. I live my own life with Peter, and I like it. He's become my family this year, and you are just a lover. Is that news to you?"

"I know that, baby. And I've feared all the time I wouldn't be able to tear you off that life with

Peter, and I am jealous."

"You knew all of it, and you're still thinking I could become a mistress to anyone who offers? Are you telling that to find some consolation? Or to just to hurt me? Are you thinking I'll choose a man with money? Nothing's easier."

"I knew. I didn't want to think about it."

"In fact, as we go on, the further we grow apart. I am happy to live with Peter. I'm so much luckier with him. Just go away. Don't you worry."

"So that's how you know who is the lucky man between me and Peter," Ilya smiled a bit.

"Peter isn't scared to introduce me to friends of his... "

"That is what I intend to do. You'll get to know all of my friends in one day. They aren't many. In case I'm not back all of them will be bankrupt."

"Well, I'm really fed up with this family argument of yours," Arcady interrupted. "Ilya, I'm getting to like you. So why do you think I may be the guarantor?"

"Arcady, ten years back you used to hold accounts in ten different banks under MTN-trading. You were the guarantor for the government. And then you were a middleman in trading. That is an impeccable reputation. So you could recommend me in ten different banks. And then we proceed upon the reference from those ten, and that should get the snowball rolling."

"Your debts are a snowball rolling," Arcady cut him short. "Where are we meeting?"

"In the airport. The day after tomorrow."

Ilya and I started going down the stairs. The front door opened on the porch into the deep twilight. Yet in the daytime the boulevard had filled up with rain was flowing with the slippery mess underfoot. But now the road was dried and widened with the lanterns' white light coming through the leaves of the trees. It was deserted, wide and resonant. And faces of the passers-by looked similar; white and frozen.

"Ilya, I think you could have found a guarantor among the bankers," I said just like that, knowing that Ilya had made his decision already.

"This isn't about the bank; I need a person with a solid reputation. There is one more thing: Arcady is a father of yours, so I can't keep running from him like a youngster."

"What's up there with that F-Group, Ilya?" I asked, taking a smoke.

"Argh... Anton. Anton is a motherfucker. I was thinking that being a merger. But it turned out someone was buying my debts from the foreign creditors. No one but Anton would wish to do so. So that's gonna be an acquisition," Ilya responded in a prose tone, as if expecting the same.

"And why exactly is this acquisition?" I asked.

"Someone wants my founder, Union-Reserve. Someone wants the money of Union-Reserve. Someone wants to switch them for service with Anton's bank, thinking they could put their hand in there unnoticed. The Central Bank is on F-Group's side. Should my bank avoid going under F-Group, the Central Bank would drive me to bankruptcy," Ilya shrugged with irritation.

"So what do you do with that?" I asked.

"I don't know. I'll have to crawl on my knees before every bank in Benelux, where I left my Foreign Currency Bonds as a pledge. And I'll keep crawling further, to meet with all my other creditors," Ilya screwed his face up.

"So how much interest will those foreign companies get in your bank?" I asked.

"I think, eighty per-cent."

"I used to like your bank in that old mansion... "

"The mansion is there to stay. All of my bank property, including the mansion, has been a long time made over as a daughter company. Everyone does it that way. So let the Central Bank drive me bankrupt as long as it likes, the creditors won't get a thing. Still there are many of those who would be bankrupt following me, I am so sorry," and Ilya stopped for a moment, thinking. "So how is Peter there? Doing fine?" he asked unwillingly.

"He wants a golden ashtray. A big one," I said.

"Why?" Ilya asked, going into his pocket for his wallet.

"It's for an Arab sheikh. They do like golden ashtrays. And then he needs a carpet and sofas... And a coffee-maker," I was speaking fast, looking at the hundred-dollar notes flash between Ilya's fingers.

Ilya, spitting out, hid his wallet, and handed me two hundreds with the words,

"Here, let him buy two ashtrays, one you bring to my bank and let him bring me a sheikh. Has Peter talked of the fountain there?"

I took the banknotes, and he could tell by my face that Peter had been talking of the fountain to me.

"Let's go to my place, baby, I am tired," said Ilya.

CHAPTER SEVEN

THE SHOOTING GROUND

In the morning I dropped by Arcady's to help him pack his things for the trip, and recalling those talks the day before he told me,

"Can't you see the difference between Peter and Ilya? Peter is just a rat. He's just adjusted to anything, be that democracy or totalitarianism, it's all the same to him, as his God is money."

"Peter is close-by to me," I stubbornly replied.

I had never seen Ilya from the same side as Arcady. Arcady told me Ilya was an aristocrat, not in his nature but in actual fact. The aristocracy had never accumulated neither wealth, nor power while serving the State. On the contrary, aristocracy was born with a sword in their hands over war and resistance to the State. The aristocracy was the absolute victory of personality against the state. And thus aristocracy is actually anti-State, and their privilege lies in their liberty.

With this spirit the feudal knight was building his castle, defending himself from the King's army. As the king sometimes had the appetite for his subjects' property, the king used to send his troops, while the feudal fought against the same. There are no other generic features. One cannot cancel history. Everyone leads his long, beaten way. So the aristocrat shall be someone who knows to fight for his honor and human dignity, without breaking up under the State machine. No matter which way you look at it, it may be either a person of reputation or man of large fortune.

Arcady said he would not be able to live like Ilya. Arcady was scared to leave his house, and would not wish to look backwards all the time.

He had seen other business people going out every day in fear, still going out there. They were getting killed. The times of the wild capitalism had gone and they had overcome their fears, becoming so rich no one would think of killing them. Arcady said he could not, and remained the slave of his fear and petty cash.

"Why are you telling me this?" I asked.

"I think Ilya is now left face to face with the Central Bank. Yes, his creditors will be against his bankruptcy, but this has to be agreed with the Central Bank, and Ilya had never licked the ass of the Central Bank. And even if he had, Ilya is nowhere near the decision-making."

In the evening Ilya and me went to his country house and somewhere short of there turned into a quiet roadway. Long and white fluffy clouds were dragging after the cars, looking even whiter in the slate-grey frozen out asphalt, narrow between the snow-banks. The road went missing in the white smokes, as if vanishing in the snows. We turned onto the country road with trees on both sides standing very close, white and frosty, and approached an abandoned shooting ground. The intact fresh snow covered the field like a tablecloth.

"Ilya, sorry, I didn't want to ask you this... but in case you refuse the merger with F-Group, will your bank go bankrupt?" I asked.

"The Central Bank wants it this way, even if all of my creditors are against the bankruptcy."

"So what happens?"

"I don't know. I'll talk to my friends now."

When we came to the shooting ground, there were three cars parked by the road. Two more cars were coming behind.

Sergey, General Manager of the aircraft factory was someone I'd known before. I also knew the others by name.

"Anna, daughter of Arcady Soloviev. I'm leaving her so that you know I'm coming back," Ilya introduced me to everyone at once.

And all of them asked how Arcady was doing.

"Like everybody else, in misery," I responded.

"Mmm... Ilya," one of them said, "I thought you were sleeping with the Armed Forces Financial Union."

"And I was thinking, with the Federal Agency for Government Communications and Information," another one said.

"That one has got too big ass," Ilya dismissed.

"So, you are with a trader... " chuckled Nicolay. "I guess as soon as you take your hand out of her panties she rushes to buy the debts of your bank."

"Nope. You've got the major debts. I'm only asking for two weeks. In the case I am late, the bank will announce my death. That may give me another three days, I hope. Should you keep holding your share of debts, there is nothing to be done without me. The blocking stake is assigned to an offshore bank. While my bank, is going bankrupt most probably. I'll have to take you with me and get to another bank. I purchased a minor bank for that purpose, named Berlin Bank. I'll exchange your debt instruments into this bank's shares, but to make it possible you have to contribute some hard cash. Get me some hard cash."

"You owe to us quite a bit already; should we lend you more money?"

"Exactly so, otherwise I won't be able to transfer you to another bank of mine. I make it a condition. I am leaving to find for us a western finance company that could be the guarantor that the Berlin Bank, where you join, does not go bankrupt."

The parting was awkward. We all left in silence.

We came back to Ilya's apartment. Ilya opened the letter from the German charity foundation given to him by Arcady, and after making a couple of calls turned to me with his face changed,

"Do you know what the BND is?"

"Foreign intelligence of Germany... What happened?"

"The head of this German foundation Paul Wogau is too much of a big-shot. It can't be that such a person would get interested with a Veterans movement that does not even exist on paper. What does he want from Vassiliev? How could Arcady get into this crap?"

"That's not hard to find out; just call him."

Ilya took the phone and froze. It wasn't easy for him to speak to Arcady. But then I heard his distant calm voice and it turned out peaceful.

During the war of 1914 Vassiliev's father was twenty years old, fresh from his grammar school. He was called up for military service and completed his officer training course. He learnt of the revolution in his country while up the line. His command kept tossing and turning from the red to the white and the other way round. He made friends with Frunze, and most probably for that reason was not assailed with doubts. When Trotsky was dethroned from the Revolutionary Military Council Chair, Frunze accepted his assignment and started gathering his own folks around him. He ordered Vassiliev out to Moscow, and the latter started working together with the Foreign Commissar Checherin. The forth division of the Red Army headquarters under Tukhachevsky at that time spared no expense on its foreign staff, especially that of Berlin. In 1924 Vassiliev's father left for Vienna as a German businessman. He bought his costume second-hand; there was nothing decent at the operational pack-house. He was a sleeper agent. From Vienna he went to Berlin, where he took roots quite easily and got married, and the same year he had a son.

While the Old World was in the trenches, in Argentina the country gentlemen started to build themselves luxurious estates and spending their money gambling, and sent their children to English schools. All that was coming from the supply of foodstuffs to the German Army during the First World War. Later President Peron promised to give a shelter to all those German officers and soldiers, in aspiration the gold of the Third Reich flows to the Argentinean banks. They say so it was, and the banks were bloated with gold, and that gold was spread right across the floor.

The family of a German businessman with a six-year-old son came to Buenos Aires from Germany by an airship of Count von Zeppelin, who was running regular flights from Friedrichshafen. Little Alexander was sent to the German school of Hindenburg in the tangerine garden. And there he made friends with Paul Wogau.

But in 1936 the dormer regiment commanding officer of Alexander's father arrived in Buenos Aires. The Vasiliev's had to dash away and return to Russia.

"So what happened to Vassiliev's father?" Ilya asked as if he knew the answer.

"He was teaching in the Military Academy of Moscow. And he was executed in 1937," Arcady replied.

"Hmm... this Paul Wogau is a friend of Vassiliev's. While they were both children. You want me to believe in this nonsense?" Ilya asked doubtfully.

"You bet. I visited Vassiliev at home yesterday, and he had a whole box of tangerines by mail."

"Arcady, could we meet Paul Wogau?"

Arcady called us back in fifteen minutes.

"He's looking forward to see us. We may stay at his house in Potsdam."

CHAPTER EIGHT

THE CLOSING DAYS

Ilya left. And those days without him were as fragile as glass on a frosty day, and restless. I was like sap with the cold, my lips blue, feeling cold and alien to myself. And with therefore totally sober eyes watching the bank of Ilya's live its closing days. I had a feeling of the clock ticking in my hands, and looking at it unable to take my eyes off the clock's twitching hand.

Ilya kept calling every day, he wanted to come back by the end of the week. He said he was tired, and wanted a good sleep at his dacha.

The terrace was frost-bound, the snow sharp and powdery like salt froze to the porch, and everything was lit with the frigid winter sun. The bright sunlight was passing through the light ice crust of the windows, and the frost-bound floor boards played in the light of silver thaw, and cracked as if breaking under my feet. The white shirts of Ilya I had washed last time were well frozen to the rope and iridescent with frost-dew in the daylight, to break away with effort and crunch like wafers, burning my fingers with cold.

Everything was wrapped in the frigid dust of non-living. I picked up a teacup to place it in the cupboard, and it fell off my hands clinking, and broke into pieces under my feet. It clove asunder as it were in an empty womb.

By the evening Victor called,

"Bunny, I thought there was someone from the Presidential administration standing up for Anton, but I am apparently mistaken. I actually failed to find out who is behind Anton; it looks like the bank has fallen on his head."

Ilya came back on Sunday night, sleep deprived and cold.

We had a coffee, and then went out to smoke on the terrace. The cigarette smoke was coming in plumes against the foggy windows turbid like a bottle of homemade vodka.

Thanks to Arcady he had managed to convince thirty banks to revoke their guarantee from Deutsche Bank pool to become stakeholders of the Berlin Bank. The rest still required some evidence.

"What kind of evidence?" I did not get.

"I think the merger of my bank with an F-Group bank is only needed to transfer Union-Reserve accounts in F-Group, to ultimately drive this F-Group to bankruptcy and get them away. And those who initiated this game in the Central Bank are actually aware I am not taking Union-Reserve to the bottom with me. I am sure of that, but how can I possibly explain this? I can't even tell this to anyone as a presumption; it's rather a shot in the dark. You fancy the way it sounds."

"That is, you actually think that F-Group appeared there only to run for its own bankruptcy?"

"Oh yes, that's usual practice. The Central Bank selects several banks to throw about some money and then drive them to bankruptcy. This is normally planned a year or more in advance. There is nothing out of common."

"Then, this means, it's the Central Bank, who's been playing against you?"

"Exactly. I did try to find out who is standing behind Anton. And there is nothing. And this blankness only means the Central Bank itself is at play."

"The blankness is not total. Why do you think so?"

"Well, there is no guarantor for Anton. I mean, there is usually a guarantor, and not for the bank that has nothing but a golden ashtray, but for the person involved. Even Peter might be guaranteed by at least three patriarchs. And Anton has none. But I've got to know that for sure," said Ilya.

"How?"

"I've got to worm into F-Group bank."

"Argh... and what if he's keeping his founders' list somewhere far away, in Kolyma?" I asked.

"I don't know what to do, baby. I've got to find out why the right to claim my bank's debt was assigned to a F-Group, and not to anybody else. And why I was not informed of the same? Why would they want to assure me there is going to be a merger? While Union-Reserve is not aware of that, and Union-Reserve have nothing against changing alongside with me for the trash hole Berlin Bank. But they still want some guarantee. And the guarantors here may be only major European banks. Deutsche Bank is upholding seventy of my creditors. Everyone wants to be where Deutsche Bank is, and Deutsche Bank wants to be with F-Group."

When hearing him, *I don't know what to do, baby,* and looking at Ilya, I suddenly felt a crashing bore, somewhat of famine. I thought Ilya was desperate. He used to know what to do, all the time.

"Wait... " I started getting across the meaning of his words. "You what, do you want to hire someone to break into the bank and heist the paperwork?"

"No. I'll have to go to that bank myself."

"Hold on... You want to put on the ski mask and break into the bank through the window?"

"I hope to get there through the door," Ilya said simply.

"And you won't go to the bank in person, will you? By yourself?!" I screamed stir-crazy into his face in a tense voice.

"You may go with me, if you want," Ilya shrugged.

"And why don't you hire someone? Or just ask Marc?" I remembered the way had so craftily hacked into the bank.

"Sure, Marc definitely will back me up there. He'll take care of the alarm system. And I'll handle the documents. We don't need to take out the bank archives and the hard disks, do we? Marc is coming along with me as... I mean, if you go, they hardly beat you up," Ilya said calmly.

I could not believe it and asked stupidly,

"Ilya, what if we get caught?"

"So what?" waved aside Ilya trivially. "No judge would ever believe the head of the bank could come to pill a bank. And then you and I, just seeking some sex and adrenaline buzz... There comes the defense attorney to speak of my senile imbecility."

I had the feeling Ilya had already made up his mind.

"Are there really no other ways but to hack into that bank?"

"We've got no time. The members' meeting is

scheduled for two days' time."

"So what you'll be looking for?"

"Some off-the-book financial schemes, something I had not seen when the paperwork for the merger was made ready."

"And how does Marc manage to switch off the alarm?"

"I've got someone who owes me in their security agency. He'd redirect the alarm signal. I'll call and give the password of my bank, and the bank of F-Group opens. And then he affects re-direction once again."

"My god... What are you doing there, Ilya? That means prison. Suppose, you won't get jailed since you got too much of a debt out there. But what happens to me?"

"Let me remind you, you wanted to be by my side, so just be there... Marc could pull you out," he said in a softer tone. "You'll make another passport and go abroad."

"And what if Marc fails to? What if something goes wrong?"

"I'll come and get you out. You have your price."

"And you get to buy the public prosecutor

altogether?" I asked, my glance freezing to his calm and cold face.

"That's where I start."

"That's not like you."

"I can't recognize myself, baby. I must be tired."

We had some cognac, and fell onto the bed, cold as a snowdrift, and immediately fell asleep.

CHAPTER NINE

THE KEY

Ilya and I went into the frosty street somewhere around eleven at night. The red glint of the cars hovering before my eyes kept flickering in the flutter of powder snow, flying into the windscreen. The pavement widely spread in the darkness, and its dirty melted waysides, appeared merged the grey facades of the Stalin-era buildings in the Garden Ring Road. The houses seemed tightly pressed to the highway, and when I came out of the car, it smelled of warm air, melting snow and gasoline.

The F-Group bank was behind an all-glass façade in the brand new building filling in gaps between two other buildings of the old housing area.

My red dress got wet with the snow sticking to my thighs. We rang at the bank doors. The door opened into the hall, spacious and resounding. Every sound echoed around like an empty cardboard box.

The guard at the reception used to know Ilya. They all knew who he was, and of the planned merger there.

Upon entry, Ilya gave a nod to him and said he came to pick up some documents. The guard asked to wait a bit to coordinate the same with his management.

Surely enough he could not get through. Ilya said he could take his time, and sent me for coffee to the night coffee shop across the road. I came back with three cups of coffee and some doughnuts. We had coffee, Ilya inquired of the guard's wife, children and dog, till the guard surrendered to sleep, his head fallen onto his elbows.

Ilya dialed the number of the security agency and said,

"Hello Pavel, this is Ilya. My vault door is jammed, the building must have sunk, and I just called the maintenance. Could you switch me off for three hours, in case they are not done, and I will call you back then?" asked Ilya giving his password.

We entered the corridor and went to the second floor to the deputy chair office. From the depths of the corridor from the opposite direction come Marc, an ex-Marine; he had been sharing the neighborhood with Ilya for ages. They have been friends for over thirty years. He was in his sixties, massive and somewhat loutish, but wonderfully handy for his age. Marc was in charge of Ilya's personal security on weekends that Ilya spent at his dacha.

While Marc was busting the safe, Ilya looked through the documents in that room and Anton's office.

The safe that Marc opened up in half an hour contained some cash, paperwork and several keys, two on each key-ring with the numbers 547 and 678 of the bank safe deposit boxes.

"Ilya," Marc called Ilya, softly, with his lips and then stopped short.

Ilya was at the doorstep with papers. Under the torchlight his face was white, just like the paper he was holding in his hands.

"Anton's dead," whispered Ilya. "There is no one behind him. His bank goes bankrupt once Union-Reserve is assigned to him."

"Why dead?"

"A few more major companies are getting transferred for service with his bank. Anton's simply a blunder-head, who would not notice them put a bomb under him. It's so grave in here, like staying in something defunct..," Ilya loosened his tie knot and drew a deep breath. "I think Anton will get killed."

"Are you sure of that, Ilya?" I could not believe it, as murder of a banker had long become unheard of.

"Well he won't get murdered... He'd get run over by a car, or get robbed near his house and won't survive. He's only got four months to live... maybe five, that is if his accountant is good enough. Marc, you go away. Take these papers and give them to Peter, let him warn the companies from this list and my own creditors, so that they keep away from F-Group. He'll do the necessary."

"Ilya, what are these keys?" I asked.

"These are the duplicate keys of a number of safe deposit boxes starting from five hundred, and those from six hundred, and those must be the numbers of personal deposit boxes. We'll see. Yet, to tell you the truth, it's all clear to me."

"Ilya, you take care," said Marc.

"Yeah, that's fine, you go away," Ilya requested, and Marc quickly disappeared in the depths of the corridor.

We went down to the vault.

Ilya took out his torch. We inserted the keys and turned them. The locks cracked. Ilya opened the door and took out the documents.

"Here, these are the companies that made their contribution to F-Group charter capital, immediately getting it back in loans," said Ilya, promptly flipping through the documents and folding them back inside. "I hope Peter could pump up the Berlin Bank charter capital with somewhat more interesting."

The vault door closed behind our backs softly and noiseless, that huge safe door. We shuddered to a halt. A trail of pale light from the corridor of the entrance lamp was getting thinner and thinner... And then went out. All that was left was the round spot of Ilya's torch in his hand. Its touch was plating rows of the safe deposit boxes filling the wall floor to ceiling with silver, and lying in flecks onto Ilya's white shirt and grey hair.

Ilya and me, we had been trapped in this vault like rats. In the deafening silence one could hear our heartbeats.

"My goodness! Are we locked in?" the icy fear rolled me up and my legs turned to jelly like snow and melted.

"They must call up the board, and promptly see what the matter is."

"And what happens to us, Ilya?"

"I think nothing. I might be forced to sign the merger agreement, or whatever else... "

"And you?"

"I'll sign everything they ask."

"What shall we do?! Oh my god what shall we do?"

"Might as well burst open the deposit boxes since we are here," said Ilya.

"Why? What are we looking for?"

The deposit boxes were fitted in their case so tightly one could hardly fit a knife edge in there. We inserted the keys again; both locks cracked simultaneously, and the door opened. We put the keys into the locks of the next box.

"There we go, is that so easy?" I asked Ilya.

"You can't imagine what they put there... Go for the bank job with a banker... You search there," Ilya nodded to the open box. "For drugs. A bottle of wine or vodka. Some kind of alcohol. And a syringe."

"Why?" I uttered unknowingly, quickly probing the heap of velvet bags in the box. My fingers felt the pricking of fine grains like buckwheat; those of petty diamonds.

"I wanna get shitfaced as soon as possible. It might be the last time. In prison one gets no chance."

Ilya was right. In the third deposit box we found some syringes and bags of heroine. After opening another few boxes we discovered a bottle of cognac.

Ilya took a comfortable seat on the floor with a bottle of cognac, and took a hundred grams of cognac through the cork with a syringe.

"You turn away."

"What are you going to do?!"

"A clyster," Ilya took the needle off the syringe and started unbelting his pants.

He got drunk in a shot. His face melted and he got a demonic glint in his eyes. I have never seen him that flyblown. His hands shivered when we were closing up the boxes.

"Once you get out of here, get me a lawyer and ambulance. Come on here with me," he said, sitting himself on the floor, cozily leaning his back to the wall and throwing back his head there. "We could take a nap."

"How can you sleep now? There?!"

"Well, I can't stand on my feet right now," Ilya smiled.

CHAPTER TEN

THE SIGNATURE

"Ilya Ivanovich, how do you do."

At the vault doorstep stood Anton, not so young and chubby, with a few rare strands of fair hair over his massive balding forehead, smooth and glossy up to the back of his neck. And his neck was rather inscribed with some wrinkles, as if he was bending his head all the time. Behind his back there was Pavel from the private agency, the man, in charge of both banks. He said,

"I am sorry I haven't called the security as agreed, instead I called the president. You are bankrupt, Ilya Ivanovich."

"You went for a bank job with your mistress?" asked Anton, having examined me from head to foot.

"You would go with her yourself."

"I didn't know your cock was still worth something," he snorted.

"Wanna check it yourself?"

"Let's go Ilya, talk to the notary."

Ilya stood up with an effort,

"My heart aches, I need a doctor. Call me the ambulance."

"You are defunct, Ilya, sign the papers and go."

"Call me the ambulance," Ilya stumbled making a few missteps.

He hardly stood on his own legs. The guard caught Ilya under his arm.

"What's up with you, Ilya Ivanovich?" asked Anton. "You aren't sick out there."

"I'm taking my treatment in Switzerland."

"He's drunk out there," softly, with his lips only the guard uttered in Anton's direction.

"He's old," the banker said between his teeth.

In the office there was a notary, bony, nervous and sleepy. Anton gave him a nod. The notary, fallen on the desk, approached his face to Ilya's, his glance flickering to examine his eyes and pupils, and then said,

"Ilya Ivanovich, could you release your breath... "

Ilya blew into his face and picked up the pen. "Everything's all right," the notary nodded to the banker and unfolded the agreement for Ilya. "Would you please sign here?"

Ilya started signing and stopped at the last page, "Let her go. And call me the ambulance, you son of a bitch. I'll put my signature once the doctor's on the threshold."

"What else?"

"Tea and a cigarette. And you fuck off, Anton."

"I would have smashed your face in, but I follow a rule, never touch the old and females. Release that whore," and he nodded at me for his guard to let go. "Ilya, you are clinging to your bank like a bloater. Give it to me, and your defense folks will survive. I could settle your debts."

"No, you could not," Ilya stood up with difficulty.

Below the windows we could hear he howl of the ambulance siren, the corridor was resounding with the medical team rapid gait. Ilya put his signature down, and the notary jerked out the agreement from under his hand.

Strung out with the night air I seemed to have plunged under water with the wet snow encrusted all over my body. I turned back to look at the bank doors. I saw the lawyer enter the bank with the blood test results. Inside the ambulance car Ilya, still drunk, was fastening his shirt.

"Ilya, anyways, you won't be able to stand against the Central Bank," I still had no clue.

"The fuck with the Central Bank talks," Ilya shrugged. "Peter must have sent over the documents to Potsdam already. And Paul Wogau will be speaking to Deutsche Bank. They will surely reach understanding. And Deutsche Bank, upon exchange of the debts for my Berlin Bank shares, will be speaking to the Central Bank."

Ilya had squeezed out everything he could from his bank prior to bankruptcy. He had been buying shares from the suspended accounts of his foreign customers, given out a Safekeeping Receipt for the gold mine and issued a couple of non-conforming bank guarantees, taken a number of loans... In a word, he had fucked out his bank to the full. On his bank balance there remained some non-liquid assets and a mountain of debts on both transactional and deposit accounts, futures and forwards, bank-to-bank loans, and hung payments to the tax authorities.

Ilya could still preserve the old mansion of his former bank, and nothing changed except for the bank signage: it was now the Berlin Bank, and its conference room was adorned with a gilded ashtray.

The Central Bank opened a credit line for Ilya's new bank.

Interview with Anna Schlegel, Author of THE DEAD BANK DIARY

I: Why the series' title is THE DEAD BANK DIARY?

A: The dead banks are the symbol of that time. So many banks expired through the national Default of 1998, and carried on after the same in a zombie way. There were too many of those. Why the Central Bank had not declared them bankrupt and let them siphon off their assets? Why the forward commitment to non-resident banks had been paid through the crisis? That is rather a rhetorical question. The Central Bank was involved with the same. Wealthy people were behind those banks.

The book series action starts back in 1998. The time of Default I keep close to my heart, I 'm still living it through. They say, the time of troubles may come and go, while the people it touched still can't stop living it through. Why so? That maybe because life in Russia deserves the case name of Russian ennui that so many classics dwell on. At the time of Default it was done with, and there came the era of overindulgence and outlawry, that is to say, the times of freedom which had never more happened ever since. I am missing those days.

I: Tell me a little about your first thriller THE DEAD BANK DIARY.

A: This is the first novel from the series. You can read each novel independently. There are the same characters. My novels are not based on a true story – that would be stupid – but you will feel the reality. The story is told from the first person; it's me. No violent crimes, or anything of the kind. No politics or 'dangerous' Russian reality. Only MONEY. Beautiful financial schemes and frauds are in each novel. I love the beautiful gray area schemes on the verge of a crime. There will be a hostile takeover of a bank or forced bankruptcy. Raider attacks on banks attract me the most.

I: What attracts you to a bank raid?

A: I saw a bank takeover with my own eyes from the beginning to the end. This had an unsuccessful ending.

But there was a moment when Victor said, *Imagine this is your own bank*.

Maybe Willie Sutton felt the same. It was no more pleasant than being in the bank at night alone.

I: Is there really a lot in your writing that has happened to you?

A: Yes, everyone in the stock market knew about it. Before default the banks fell down as a house of cards. Banks were pumped up with money and went bankrupt very easily. It was the period of wild capitalism, and I was lucky that time has passed through me.

I: You write you have been sick with millions...

A: Of course, big and easy money is like a drug. I hid this disease a long time, as alcoholics or addicts do. And then I used as well. Maybe I was lucky that I remained without work. I also realized that I would never get a job. What was important earlier to me lost its sense. I had a hungry look.

At that time I was mixed up. People had lost their former life. It was easy to get acquainted with everyone: a minister, a diplomat, a vice-president of the bank... I felt that time was not so long. That crazy time would leave as fast as a river. It would take the big fish away. It would go down to the depths. Already that time has gone. That time you could catch a big fish with your bare hands. I have nothing to regret.

I: Are these frauds real?

A: Yes, they are true. But to accomplish this you need an insider in the bank. Better someone on the bank board. Or you must get a lot of money to fall down the bank.

I: Is money the main thing in your novels?

A: Yes: if you're wondering how to get money out from thin air, the smell of money, how to reverse off-balance money, how to break banks, then my novels are for you. I write all about the money. The reader will always know what to expect.

I: The main hero of the series is Victor; meanwhile the hero of the first novel is Ilya. Why so?

A: Books are written in memory of Victor, a retired

Foreign Intelligence Service officer and a fraudster. I was lucky to meet him. He died more than ten years ago. At the heart of all the novels will be my memories of him.

The hero of the first thriller and the following novels is Ilya, the bank's chairman. He is in his seventies. I imagine that some readers will be turned off by his age. But heroes come from anywhere. Writers sometimes say that characters find themselves. Ilya is a real person. He had become a hero unexpectedly for me. But I cannot tell who this character really is. In any case, all the heroes I've written about are real people. Default time in 1998 has made its own characters. They have been called the children of default. In real life they look like characters in a novel. It seems to me that the real life is much more interesting than any fiction.

I: Your novels are realistic, aren't they?
A: Exactly. While I worked as a market middleman, I made some digital recordings. That's a lot of hours of negotiations. I did not make these recordings for my safety. There is no danger if you know the rules of

Russian deals. Did I feel that very sharply at the time? I realized that the time of default would pass away. And to build a business from scratch would be impossible. I felt everything would come to an end very quickly. There were crazy days. I do not know why I've made these recordings. It was done by intuition. My novels have begun from these records. Some conversations were so interesting that they were included in the text with a few changes.

But the novels are not realistic. They are not like 'Liar's Poker' by Michael Lewis, for example. My thrillers are completely in line with the laws of the novelistic genre. Here there is intrigue, the heroes find out something unexpected about themselves, and there is a twist in the end. That is why in the first thriller I have got a US Federal Reserve Bond, face value one million dollars, issued in 1934. A very beautiful fake.

I: Was this bond real?
A: Oh, yes. Some fakes arrived on the market from various backgrounds. One of the most plausible stories says that a box with these bonds was taken out from Germany at the end of World War II. Boxes are gone

around the world. So the Fed decided to devalue them. Dresdner bank issued a letter about its ability to accept the bonds. There was one thing: each bond had to have the Treasury Certificate, Global Immunity and Gold Bullion Certificate. But there were not. It's just a beautiful story. They say also that one of boxes taken out from Germany had been opened by one of our drunk generals. But it is known that some the European banks accepted these bonds as a deposit. I haven't held this bond in my hands. I had only a high-quality digital copy. It's a terrific document. And I have seen the parent papers. The stories about these bonds are so various... I told a one in my novel.

In fact, the story of a document from Dresdner Bank seems true. Once a casual acquaintance from special service said that not so many years ago, he unloaded trucks with trophies from German museums, which were brought from Moscow to Tomsk. There were leather-bound folios with engravings. They have not been packed and were unloaded without inventory. They were frozen in the thirty-degree frost.

I: Do you have any acquaintances from special

service?

A: Just a few. These are the people from whom I try to be as distant as possible. But time goes on, things change. If someone said that I was seeking an 80-year-old professor, former officer of the NKVD (the People's Commissariat of Internal Affairs, the forerunner of the KGB), and we would have absolutely similar views on life, I would never believe it.

I: Is he Ilya?

A: Partly. Outwardly of course. He was a handsome, 6'5 feet tall, accustomed to getting any woman he wants.

I: And so your hero is in his seventies...

A: Yes, Ilya would not be the chairman of the bank if he was younger. It would be not plausible. But he is a strong hero. He loves risk. Do not worry, the main hero never will die and will not be ill at all. And what the hell can I do if this hero appeared, living his own life? He is stronger than me.

I: Your novels are written from the first person. You are the storyteller and the hero. How much

truth is in your words?

A: Not a lot. But I am the reliable storyteller. You can trust me. There are two main heroes: Ilya and me. There is a main hero in two characters. I am the hero who could not pull off the plot. I am the type of hero who is called 'a magnet for shit'.

And Ilya, on the other hand, is the bastard. He breaks all the rules. He cannot be understood. He is not cruel himself. He has his logic. To be with Ilya is like making a deal with a devil. He doesn't need a victory or money. For him there is neither good nor evil. He simply stretches a hand and undresses who he needs. He can undress FSB (former KGB) or the church. He does not care.

Ilya is an outstanding character. I am glad that this hero has found me, and let me to write first four novels, and I hope there will be new one. He is inexhaustible. It's not just a thriller but a love story.

I: Tell me about yourself as a hero.

A: I'm a free trader, without any work, without a family and without any attachments. I've got a father.

We met each other when I was a child, and I am happy with him. My heroes have also no family. They have a past, but I do not describe it. They simply live day by day. Each novel is one month in the lives of the characters. A story begins wherever it catches them. There are no memories.

I go on my way following the big money. It attracts me. I am infected with crazy millions. The people like me are few. Time has changed. It seems my kind doesn't exist anymore. I have an outgoing nature. But I love going after millions. It seems I will die on the run. I think I'm going mad. Where will I be on my way? Let me.

I: Are all of you heroes swindlers?

A: Yes, they are ordinary people. There are no good guys. There are no murderers. Losers just stay without money. Money is the most humane weapon.

I: Why are they so?

A: I have the answer in my second novel FOR THOSE IN THE SHADE. They are that way by nature. They just eat each other. Sometimes literally. And there is nothing to do about it. It is simply a life. There is a beautiful and convincing psychological theory about it. It's founder is a Russian prof. Porshnev.

I: You have a philosophical degree. Are there other philosophical theories?

A: Nietzsche and Russian philosopher Berdyaev are closer to me. But in my novels there are no long conversations. My heroes do not sit down with a cup of coffee. Each novel has a theme and a counter-theme. For example, the person is against the tyranny of absolute power, or against the law of necessity.

I: How about you? Are you a badass hero?

A: Of course. But I found it hard to write about myself as a badass. It was real hell. Good guys seem boring and unrealistic to me.

I: How much do you write about Moscow?

A: Not a lot. It's so funny to see how Hollywood films present Moscow as a dangerous city. Moscow does not differ from a European megalopolis.

But of course it is Moscow. I write about that time

when the city was flooded with fantastic money. All was on sale: oil, gas, diamonds, public debts... The city breathed big money. I often write about it.

That time has gone, and the city was paralyzed without money. During that time empty buses were passing through downtown. And again Moscow began to choke with million-strong oil contracts, federal programs and cheap bank guarantees. Also there were offers of high yield private placement programs with sonorous names of the Top 100 European banks. With mad percentages. They had nostalgia for those days that had recently fallen. They smelled of the quiet life.

I: Don't you think Moscow is a dangerous city?

A: I understand your question. Well, as dangerous as an arms dealer? Maybe now there is some interest in Moscow, but I would not like to write more about Moscow as a landscape. Of course, my main hero has a bodyguard.

Is Russia dangerous? No. People with ideology are dangerous. Rich Russians have not got it. Ideology is for the poor. The poor cannot make a rich state.

I: Have you had a hard life? Are you writing much about yourself?

A: Not much. But I try to explain what a person feels after he has been gobbled up by a city such as Moscow.

Interview with Anna Schlegel, Author of THE PRINTS ON THE SNOWS OF YESTERYEAR

I: This is your third novel. This is about another fraud?

A: In this novel there is a very beautiful fraud. The bank is fully transferred in a bank double. From this, all that remains is just the name and a heap of debts.

Here are the same heroes: the chairman of the Board, Ilya, his 'shadow' – the former vice-president Peter, and me, the jobless trader.

I: Is your hero forced to look for a bank double?

A: In the first novel Ilya has left as deposit of Foreign Currency Bonds into several small European banks under their guarantee. This step becomes his mistake. Who could know that Foreign Currency Bonds would be worthless? It is the collapse. Nobody expects it. The largest Russian banks take out credit secured by the government securities, Foreign Currency Bonds, Eurobonds and debt of a London club. They become worthless in a flash, worth less than ten percent of their face value. Russian banks lose a hundred million dollars every minute on this fall. The European banks at the same time put the requirement surcharge cost of these bonds which were revalued to market losing their price. The novel begins at Ilya's bank which is on the verge of bankruptcy, wlth the words: *The Bank, facing bankruptcy, fell out of the hands like a snowball rolling downhill to flatten everything under its weight.* Thus he is forced to look for a bank double.

I: Could this fraud happen anywhere?

A: Yes, banks-doubles are used worldwide. I write about Moscow, but Moscow reality is not intrusive in my thrillers. You can read it and not feel, that it takes place in Moscow. Snow, KGB and the spies – all in the past. Snow has remained.

I: You say your heroes are unpunished, aren't they?

A: Absolutely. I write about real financial grey schemes, that have been used in the banks already. None have resulted in criminal charges. One time in Moscow several major banks on the verge of bankruptcy moved to banks doubles.

I: You mention the story of two American spies, Sarant and Barr...

A: Yes. They are known for the Rosenberg case. They had been taken from the USA to the Soviet Union. They became the founders of the microelectronics industry in Russia. Their story is very interesting. But I write more about Lieutenant General Oleg Chembrovsky (his name is changed in the novel), who worked with them. He stayed on at the beginning of the USSR Space Defense Program. After the Default he searched for money for a Military Electronics Research Institute. And... my friend decided to create the WWII Veterans' Movement in his honor.

I: This Veterans' Movement is not just in your imagination?

A: It's not, no. It happened before my eyes from the idea. My friend could not take none cent for this Movement. Maybe it was the wrong time for this. But he got to celebrate Victory Day in the Column Hall of the House of Unions, between the Kremlin and the Bolshoi Theatre. It's a lucky day. That Movement began as the usual scam: prominent people were included in a list of founders they knew nothing about. For the meeting my friend made a shuttle operation and invited useful persons to meet each other...

Oleg Chembrovsky died soon. Every year the date is commemorated in his institute. That's why my novel is called THE PRINTS ON THE SNOWS OF YESTERYEAR.

I: Is there a philosophical theory behind the book?

A: Here is Nicholas Berdyaev's idea on the origin of Aristocracy. Just in a nutshell. Aristocrats are not born but made. Aristocracy is anti-State. Its privilege is freedom. It's an absolute triumph of the individual over Government. So the feudal knight built his castle. He defended himself from the King's army. Kings used to have to rob his sovereign, and the King sent his army. The feudal knight fought with the King's army and won. Aristocracy has no other generic features.

You may also be interested in novels by Anna Schlegel

THE DEAD BANK DIARY SERIES

THE DEAD BANK DIARY

Book One of The Dead Bank Diary Series

ISBN: 9780986174919
ASIN: B00OPAZQMI

FOR THOSE IN THE SHADE

Book Two of The Dead Bank Diary Series

ISBN: 9780986174964
ASIN: B014Q92DE6

SOME DAY I`LL HIT A BANK

Book Four of The Dead Bank Diary Series

ISBN: 9780998185323

THE FROZEN DEBT

Book Five of The Dead Bank Diary Series

ISBN: 9780998185309

MY GOD IS MONEY

Book Six of The Dead Bank Diary Series

Coming Soon

THE DEAD BANK DIARY

Book One of The Dead Bank Diary Series

by Anna Schlegel

ISBN: 9780986174919
ASIN: B00OPAZQMI

The rats living on the refuse of the bank backyard stay
full at all time

This is not a robbery. A bank is taken with all its guts: accounts, debts, points of exchange, the staff to the last secretary, the building. This is beautiful and clean fraud.

I was out of work, while all around you could smell millions, even in the air outside. It was an unforgettable smell of public debt, oilfields, gold, bank guarantees, diamonds... I wanted to breathe in the air of easy cash Moscow, to revel and roll in this air. I could feel the smell of money in the wind on my face. This air was used to make up funds overnight, to make a fortune, to go rack and ruin and then grow rich again. It was going free across the wreckage of the sold out Soviet empire.

I was asked to help redeem the debts of a bank. The insider man at the bank held the post of Vice President.

A bit of danger and a bit of love.

FOR THOSE IN THE SHADE

Book Two of The Dead Bank Diary Series

by Anna Schlegel

ISBN: 9780986174964
ASIN: B014Q92DE6

You may live your whole life without getting to know who you are, and sometimes this is for the better

It was a bank robbery, however this time the gunmen came not for the cash but for the bank itself, and all that followed happened faster than a domino knockdown.

The bank was bankrupted professionally.

Bad debts of the Third World countries, Cuba, Zimbabwe, Morocco, and The Congo have been returned on the bank's balance sheet. Once, the bank sold the debts to itself, to an offshore company.

Who did this?

The banker finds out the bank in Amsterdam... and has taken it over completely.

SOME DAY I`LL HIT A BANK

Book Four of The Dead Bank Diary Series

by Anna Schlegel

ISBN: 9780998185323

The bomb lives to its internal time

My life became lonely and monotonous, almost mechanical in nature, with a mechanism akin to a ticking bomb. It could be ticking for days and weeks, quiet and imperceptible, to blow up everything around at the right time.

This way common folks used to live in the past, bakers and shoemakers. They lived their lives until the revolution burst out. It was their time. And then they went out the door of their bakery and shoe shop for good to take the ministry chairs and cut the heads off the aristocracy, by weaving plots and intrigues. I knew I will not miss my time.

It seemed to me I could go on for another ten years, and one day stumble on a terse line in the newspaper and realize: my time has come.

THE FROZEN DEBT

Book Five of The Dead Bank Diary Series

by Anna Schlegel

ISBN: 9780998185309

When totally nude have a look, maybe you still got the shoulder loops

One morning he stayed bare-ass, there was no money, no name, no wife, and nothing left... just his shoulder loops.

MY GOD IS MONEY

Book Six of The Dead Bank Diary Series

by Anna Schlegel

Coming Soon

———————————————————

A bank is like a condom, you can only use one at a time

The rats are perennial, they'll exist till the end of times, wealthy and miserable, in the wild or in prison, through any shift in power or regime change, be that capitalism or communism, and nothing would ever alter them as they could adapt for any environment and their world of invisible omnipresence is well protected by their God, and no one would get out of His hand since their God is money.

SPY & FINANCIAL THRILLER

THE SLEEPER SERIES

MONEY CAN`T LIE

Book One of The Sleeper Series

ISBN: 9780998185330

ON MYSELF FOR LITTLE MONEY

Book Two of The Sleeper Series

Coming Soon

AUTHOR'S NOTE

There are no agents and no offices furnished with the electronics, it is free of everlasting arguments with the management and those talks of the crummy salaries.

He's an agent with no support, and he's got nothing on his hands... But then why, if he is a respectable banker in a European bank?

ABOUT THE SLEEPER SERIES

These are the books about someone I met in Berlin, and four days later I had to become his wife and his backer-up, the second key to the deal, the duplicate. It would not have happened if he had not turned into a transient target for the secret services, a mere bargaining chip. He was sold out as a long sleeping Russian agent.

The deal to which Vlad was a shadow partner was tied up.

This deal was about the discharge of foreign debts of several countries in Africa via a number of embassies and ministries, oil companies and stock trading businesses, through the German and Swiss banks... It involved over a hundred different partners, functionaries and security officials, company leads and multiple agents. And they were all hidden behind a bunch of middlemen. This deal was made of personal contacts and handshakes, of non-committal talks and of pure air. Once materialized, the deal incorporated proper ironware and Swiss-clock precision.

Who would not wish to hold this kind of deal in their hands? They were so many. It could make a perfect channel for arms or diamond trafficking.

However the people were the main asset of that deal. So it took us a while to realize in the wrong hands it could play on one occasion only, and that would be to knock out just a single man.

If only we had known this, it would be clear there was no coincidence, there was no token money in that big a game, and every player was worth a lot. Seven digits were invested into this deal takeover, and should they fall onto us in a banking package it would have crushed us like a block of concrete.

That time we were not aware of this. Vlad and I were making time pass in an empty house in the suburbs of Berlin along with vodka and cakes, trying to figure out why the hell the British intelligence had started to look out for Vlad as a Jewish mom?

They say, nothing bands people better than fear, neither love nor hatred.

These novels are not based on actual events but you can still scent the reality in every word.

MONEY CAN`T LIE

Book One of The Sleeper Series

by Anna Schlegel

ISBN: 9780998185330

Should there be three pieces of crap this is of the British intelligence classic

One day there happened what may happen to a sleeping agent, he was burnt by the same intelligence he worked for. He expected to be arrested and suddenly realized all those things he felt overwhelming for the last week were nothing but seeming true. And in reality it was all quite different, and he had to save not his neck but the operation to which he was a shadow partner.

This deal left no legible trace. It was just like a woman always staying with somebody else in her pursuit of money. It was made of thin air, of powerful links, of noncommittal talks and handshakes. In this deal every cent was lying in someone's hands. So not knowing the hand that handed this cent over to some other hands one could learn nothing at all, and the whole thing turned to be a number of bulging bubbles of virtual money that disappeared from bank accounts with a single keystroke. It became the reality pulling in to death.

So many people wanted to hold that deal in their hands.

Therefore he understood nothing would happen to him there, he could just walk out with no glance back since he knew so well all those counterparties involved in this operation, and these people could sense something went wrong from miles away and could read it by his walk, there was no need to warn them, they would scatter away on their own and hideaway like rats. And the deal would vanish alongside with them, flowing like sand between his fingers.

If someone wanted to hold down that deal nothing wrong could happen to him. He just had to walk into the street. But then, what if he was mistaken?

ON MYSELF FOR LITTLE MONEY

Book Two of The Sleeper Series

by Anna Schlegel

Coming Soon

The British intelligence cannot compromise its integrity, it will adhere to its principles like in the old times of rock`n`roll. And it's damn good to look at it working... but then it's scary to see it work against yourself.

He was not worth a straw to the intelligence, a mere sleeper, a small coin. One day he felt behind his back there was someone else, someone a big shot of so high value they could not afford to lose him. Who could that be, a recent turncoat? He had no idea.

He could only see a trace of him barely-there, just a tip. And they were seeking to ward the trail off, not just by drawing it aside as now it appeared leading straight to him. So that everything would point to him.

The trace would be lifeless, of beautiful classics and as much stone-dead.

ABOUT THE AUTHOR

I was born in Moscow. I studied at the Moscow State University at the Philosophical faculty. I got a PhD in philosophy and stayed without work and without money. The financial crisis began. Some years I was looking for a work, but took it easy. I was a securities trader in an investment company by chance. And then there was the default in 1998. I was without work again.

This was my best time. I became the financial middleman of off-market private transactions. I had nothing. I have been looking for too-big deals. But then there was a time that it was quite possible for me to be the middleman in the sale of a Libyan oil tanker or the sale of aircrafts abroad. I got sick of conducting multi-million dollar transactions and lost all sense of reality.

I met Victor. He was a retired Foreign Intelligence Service officer. He was a magnificent fraudster. I understand how strange it sounds. But at that time before the Yeltsin decree in February 1996 the Intelligence Service was pumped up by money. And Intelligence Service officers one by one began to hold the post of deputy chairmen of the bank. It had happened overnight. Certainly, I could say: he was a magnificent financier, but... to call him as a financial fraudster would be more truthful.

Capturing the bank was in my sights. The insider of the bank was the vice-president of the bank. I write about his capture almost unchanged. Victor would be recognized by his conversations. Before leaving, he left me his three passports... So I do not know his real name. There were no closed doors for him. He had friends from the federal agency for government communication and information and from the board of directors of Deutsche Bank. All kinds of people.

Years passed. Victor is long gone. And there are fewer middlemen.

I feel myself to be on the way out. The whole generation is on the way out as well, those who are described as robbing the country.

I like those who robbed the country, and I'm pleased how it was done. They were really talented financiers, nothing worse than financiers on Wall Street. They left the country and have taken the money with them.

Since then, Moscow's air did not smell of millions any longer. But it seemed to me, it was still in the depths of my house between a pile of white shirts.

Now there are no more financial middlemen. The young have got jobs first. They receive a salary at the end of the month, and seem to have already forgotten the smell of crazy millions. It's like being drunk. There's a dizziness from it... They did not want to breathe this air. They did not want to poison their lives. They earned their money. They had wives, children, dogs, cars, which it is necessary to care of... Their heads have been overflowing with thoughts of petty cash.

Then the middlemen were old. And I stayed with them. Therefore, the heroes of my novels are in their sixties.

For the former friends who stayed in the stock market I became infected. No, I just died. And I have been smelling of sweet cadaveric decay.

It seemed to me that I was among the dead. And

it felt really bad for me as a living being. But I shared their way of thinking. I was the same as they were. Ridiculous and old-fashioned, useless clutter, rubbish. Market garbage.

My friends were precisely the same as a middle-aged gentleman.

Sometimes I catch a strange look at myself, but then forgot about it. The metropolis cleaned me from their memory. There was no need to be as nice as kind people who talk with clients and colleagues daily. I had a different way of talking. My talking always led to a deal. And in case it didn't, I would give the finger and immediately forget the useless person as if shaking off dust. And that's all.

I have nothing to regret. I had nothing to blame myself for. Dogs wouldn't blame themselves for their dog's life, would they?

I could not return back to the stock market. It has changed. Brokers, buyers, and sellers have been changed. They all had grown up a little. They have got each other for 0.1 percent interest, ready to set their ass to everyone at 0.5 percent, and would sell their own mother at one percent. I could not do that. The market has kicked me out as garbage.

And the old, among whom I used to be, are gone. The reality of small money has burnt out people around me as fire burns wood. Sometimes it seems to me that I have gone mad, that I live in the world turned inside out. Sometimes I would like to be like anyone... to have a rest, eat, dress, buy a car...

But I can't do it. It would be a living death.

It seems to me I would lose days and years and end up in devastation and poverty. And I would lose the scent of money, and the skill ... I clung to the sale of oil, diamonds, and bank guarantees, though I'm sure that it was simply thin air and there was nothing behind it. Sometimes I woke up and thought that all was not with me. But I lived and breathed the air of millions. It was my life. In my life I gained money from thin air. Emptiness is a magnet for me.

Now I have got nothing. I do not care. I like my life. I like to go for millions. It's impossible to stop me. I might be put down like a mad dog.

And I still have a sense of money. I can smell the street's air and say that the market has changed. It smells as sharp as the smell of fresh bread from a bakery in the frost.

FINANCIAL THRILLER

THE DEAD BANK DIARY

SERIES

SOME DAY I`LL HIT A BANK

By Anna Schlegel

BOOK FOUR

The bomb lives to its internal time

CHAPTER ONE

SAND HAZE

Tallinn, May 2001

One fucking day I ended up with a million dollar on my account. This was pretty much the outcome of my lunatic life. Everything looked the way I had thieved it.

Who would ever believe a jobless trader, who had long ago forgotten the looks of a hundred dollar, that he had not thieved anything? No one would. I would never believe it myself. Oh, I wish I could help myself to a million bucks so much there! And then spread it out into several offshore companies and run off, free and easy, the way birds fly away. But I could not do it.

In reality it all seemed a deal. It was nothing out of common. This money was intended to be pocketed by one of Fin Holdings bank founders, without a trace, so that no one in his bank could find out. And what can be more convenient than just tell this money had been stolen by an offshore firm manager who then escaped abroad with it? Why not do it this way?

Of that banker I actually knew nothing but his name. There were no links between us whatsoever. The bank security would scrape around for evidence, down to my panties and would not find any links neither with their bank nor with that banker. Of course the bank would file a lawsuit against me and all my accounts would get blocked within a week. This bank could afford to go into litigation with an offshore firm. And for me that was nothing but a minor nuisance. Some time will pass, maybe six months or less, and then I could give this money back to the banker in exchange for Peter. I would retain a certain amount to recompense myself for all the trouble.

Should I not return the money, I would never see Peter again. The banker made me understand he would keep an eye on Peter. In the language of that weird deal it meant Peter is retained as security just in case I get away with the money. The banker did not say anything about it, just a couple of words on the phone that he intended to keep Peter within reach, but anyway this was all quite clear.

I was hoping it could work out all right if I properly meet his requirements. It was not difficult to do. It was good enough to diffuse that million so it leaves no trace and then lie low, the latter being pretty easy as well, all the more so, as I guessed the bank security was reporting to the same banker.

So I was a thief on the run with a view to get into prison in case they find me. And what did it mean to be named a thief for me, taken I had been living on no money for years? No biggie. I was a helpless idiot one could kick in the arse easily and tell, "Here you go, have a run, baby".

What could I lose there? Nothing really. I had nothing at all. It was all the same to me what my friends and acquaintances might think of me. The majority of those would just envy. As to the others, honestly, I would just tell them to get lost. And then, who would ever get to know of this thievery? The banks prefer to keep quiet when money gets stolen. But still I had that father of mine, Peter. And Peter stayed in his apartment in Tallinn. He said he would live there till the dust settled.

Why could not I just go to the countryside? This was my initial thinking.

Marc brought me to an old house at the sea coast, about a hundred kilometers from Tallinn where I was supposed to spend a few months.

We were driving in twilight along the shore. The road, white and pecky for the wind was hardly twinkling in the headlight beam like fish scale. The smooth brown boulders along the sea shore with a touch of gray moss looked rather like sugar-topped Easter cakes. On the other side of the road there were dunes as far as the eye could reach, that vanished in the fog of the sand haze.

"The bank would hire a retired intelligence professional," Marc was saying, peering through the sand haze and wiping his perspired forehead with a bright handkerchief dangling on his neck. "To start with, he would be looking for your fingerprints on all the dicks of the bank board. You are a female. Under that logic you could be someone's girlfriend, a girl who stole the money for someone in the bank. And when he finds no one there he would finally do what he was hired for, that is following the money trace. Could you light me a cigarette," Marc asked me again. "The tracker would come to Peter. Or he may not come. But he would surely find out everything about Peter and... also find out that Ilya at first kicked Peter out, hammer and tongs, and later hired Peter for a month into his new bank so that within that month the bank charter capital tripled. This will lead them to Ilya..."

"Oh my God, is it so easy to link Ilya to Peter?" I wondered lighting a cigarette for Marc and taking a smoke next to him.

"The main thing, it is not so easy to link you to Ilya," Marc took a deep draw on his cigarette; one could see he had been thinking this over many times. "I hope they won't find you here right away. And what are you thinking of it all?"

"I don't know. It's a deal. I got to exchange that freaking million for Peter. In case Ilya manages to work the money and make a million and a half out of this million over a short time that would be not so bad," I answered, having some second thoughts.

"Nope. This is no deal. There can be no exchange. The banker is to be killed. Could you light me a cigarette," Marc told this matter-of-factly, and I felt cold of this simplicity.

I thought I would never get used to the kind of man Marc seemed to be and the kind he actually was.

Marc was huge, with his paunched body and his drunken face, soft and doughy like wet bread. When I'd seen him for the first time he seemed to me rather invisible and commonplace, somewhat like an insurance agent or a bookkeeper. His lips were wet and when smiling he bared all his teeth, small and fishlike sharp. He had watery eyes that never smiled. And his loutish gaze would instantly send you spinning away.

For him the most spine-chilling things were just a matter of routine that he lived with daily. But he was fond of life. And he looked filled up and insatiable at the same time. One could see he would keep throwing up to eat some more.

I felt easy with Marc as if I had known him all my life, the way I know myself. Maybe so, through the smoke of his cigarettes I could sense a faint smell of the campfire. And this smell was always with him, and for me this was just like the smell of home where along with cold I would get away with fear, as the promise of a quiet day.

Marc was an old friend and a bodyguard of Ilya. I had been dating Ilya, the head of a small Moscow bank, for about two years now and I used to come to his country house at weekends. Marc had a house nearby Ilya`s, so Marc was always close by.

"Kill the banker, Marc?" I inquired, transfixed with a cigarette in my hand, thinking I must have heard amiss.

"Yes," Marc nodded. "You are not thinking of this now, but after some time you'll be just like me. Believe me there. The banker is twisting your arms. There is only one way to stop it, kill the man."

"Marc... " I started, lighting another cigarette for him but he cut me short.

"Do you really think this banker has offered you a deal there? Don't you be so naive. This is arm-twisting. At this point the banker himself does not intend to rip you off. But life would make him do so. That happens all the time. He is forcing himself into a corner. And with the person who is twisting your arms, the only way is kill him... Ilya also said there is no need to play anybody's game; you need your own game. Are you frozen there? Would you give me that cigarette now? The banker would find it easier to lock you up.

That way he wouldn't have to worry... Don't you understand what you've put your foot into?"

"You must be right. I'm stuck there," I nodded, lighting up my cigarette after him.

"It's not a big deal. You'll stay in prison for a while, make friends with some wealthy people... " Marc dissolved into noiseless laughter. "Don't you tell me anything for now. We'll talk about it in a month's time. After a couple of days I'll come to see how you are doing here. I just told you this, and you've heard it. That's all for now. Have a look over there," Marc nodded in the village direction one could hardly nick in the haze. "Here they got a library, a polyclinic and a post office. The internet is that side."

In the distance an old stone house came in sight, submerged into the dunes up to its windows the way tombstones get buried, it was with no porch, with a low brick fencing and a garden, it looked as an abandoned bird nest. Through the bare branches of the apple trees I could see the poor household of the backyard, with a downfallen greenhouse of tattered polyethylene, and a pooped chicken-run, and the insides of the broken-backed garage as if turned inside out with its gate wide open hosting an old red Yugo car.

This used to be a house of a blue-water sailor. For everyone there I was his niece. And he was at sea. I came to live there to take care of his old tomcat. I had no cell phone, and in case something happened I was supposed to send a letter using the ship's mail so that Marc could read it.

The house was vacant and stale. There was a lot of furniture, yellow and unpolished items of the sixties, of which it felt even a bigger void. Or it only seemed so for to the ceiling beaded with plywood painted in blue. The plywood was buckled and the paint peeled off baring the black nail heads. That way in autumn yellow trees stand under the heavy blue skies, and here one could feel the same autumn void, that sharp smell of it. A floor-lamp on a bamboo leg bearing sun-bleached and worn-out yellow silk was shaking of every footstep scattering blurred thick light. Everything around had a slight touch of decay.

The house was located in two kilometers from the village, close to the shore with a rotten wood pier. Should someone approach the house I could see him from a far off. At the pier Marc started the motor boat.

"That's it," Mark said making fire in the mantelpiece. "Should someone find you in this asshole it would be the guy from the bank."

"It seems my life has got flushed down the toilet right here," I uttered looking around.

"There is no flush toilet this side, just a wooden outhouse with a sinkhole for the crap," Marc snicked and said goodbye.

Marc left, and I followed him with my eyes still not getting I was left alone there to find solutions on my own.

After shaking the sand off the bed sheets, I had some vodka, and when falling asleep I was thinking, *Oh my God, where is the time when I used to borrow a hundred dollar every time we talked of those multi-million deals? I was so much accustomed to fighting for every cent and moon over big money. It felt so very bad without that rat race!*

In the morning I had a coffee with oatmeal biscuits and it tasted gritty. It seemed the time stood still as if I had been living there for years. It was all the same to me.

Peter had taught me to live in no hurry. Inside I had everything properly calibrated like clock-work, as if an invisible hand d started an iron mechanism and the rhythm of it was in my blood so I could not stop it anymore. This work was making me live in a hard fisted and mean-hearted way, ready In the wings for my proper time.

When would this time come? What would it be like? It did not matter. I knew so very well I would not miss it. I knew it for sure. So I did not worry. And I did not feel upset looking into my mirror to see on the left of my nose the wrinkle lowering the edge of my lip for ever. I was able to put on my worn-out shoes without much sorrow. I'd learnt to wait for my money with a lot of patience and calm. This way the mechanism of a ticking bomb would go on quiet and imperceptible. And I knew I would not miss the proper time.

The thing was, to strike a single monetary operation one had to be ready for it for years, every day and every minute. The deal was to be searched for with due time to lie in wait. So this way I was living there, waiting, ready to snatch it like a dog catches hold of a thrown bone, on the fly, and then run away.

For me it was so easy I was ready to never leave my house and do nothing about it. I could tell everyone to get lost and just stay there waiting dumbly, just like this time. It seemed I could endlessly listen out for the delicate squeak of the wind through the glass in the old window frame, for the quiet steps of the old Siamese tomcat, for the crispy knock of the clock.

Sometimes I was thinking I could die and never see anything coming.

But then I really knew what I was waiting for. And I knew I would see it coming, sooner or later. And I knew the way it should be when my time comes. I would always recognize my time coming. I had no idea how, but I had developed that animal-like power of scent. One should sense his time well in advance. That way one may feel the smell of the coming rain in the air. And I must have smelled it already, inhaling a good deal, as if it had touched my face...

I would just rouge my lips and go out the door to never come back.

Anna Schlegel has a degree in philosophy. She was Securities trader before the recession. The last ten years she has been involved in off-market private transactions as a middleman in Moscow.

She writes in genre of financial thriller.

Anna lives in Novi Sad, Serbia.

CONTACTS INFORMATION

For information about the author, please visit TheDeadBankDiary.com, thedeadbankdiary@gmail.com

For information about the published books, please contact Schlegel Press Association at schlegelpressassociation@gmail.com

Anna Schlegel

www.ingramcontent.com/pod-product-compliance
Lightning Source LLC
Chambersburg PA
CBHW070933130626
46555CB00001B/415